W9-BBE-739

My Father
IMMORTAL

By the same author

Mercedes Nights
Wolf-Dreams
Nightreaver

My Father

·IMMORTAL·

MICHAEL D. WEAVER

ST. MARTIN'S PRESS ■ NEW YORK

Design by Judith Stagnitto

Library of Congress Cataloging-in-Publication Data

Weaver, Michael D.
      My father immortal.

      I. Title.
PS3573.E179M9   1980   813'.54   88-29809
ISBN 0-312-02617-X

First Edition
10 9 8 7 6 5 4 3 2 1

for Angel

My Father
IMMORTAL

Prologue

■ ON MOCCASINED FEET, she crept along burnished metal hallways, each soft thud tightening the knot in her stomach, loosening another strand of her unraveling nerves. Her breathing thundered in the silence; when she swallowed, she felt as if she swallowed her heart. But she moved, like slow lightning through an invisible maelstrom, and she reached the door through which she was forbidden to pass.

She stopped and fell back against the wall, breathing deeply and closing her eyes. Control, she thought. Control.

Behind the door were her children, her twins, Daniel and Monica: her children the damned, two years old, theoretically innocent, harmless, but you'd think they had the plague. She could still feel them inside her, shifting, kicking, then torturing her as they'd clawed out into the world of light. She'd been the first to give birth, and she'd done it with no help but that of her two pregnant sisters; the rest of the family had already disowned the infants, even then, before they'd been born.

Four days later, Tiffany had helped Jan's little boy into the uncaring metal world. Then Rachel had had triplets.

Six damned, innocent lives.

She punched her access code into the door's keypad. The hydraulics hissed softly, and Tiffany sighed. No alarms; Jan, at least, hadn't been caught. Thank God. Daniel stirred in his sleep as Tiffany entered the room.

"Mommy?"

"Shhh. Here, take your blanket. Come here." She scooped up the boy in one arm, then lifted Monica from her cot; the baby girl sniffed, then smiled in her sleep.

Daniel woke fully and stared at her with his big, blue eyes. Could he know? she wondered. Could he understand what was happening?

Passing lightly now, sylphlike, through the halls, she wondered how her children, the laser rifle strapped to her back, the dense memory cubes, and the laser pistol at her belt—how it all—could feel so light. Like feathers, or maybe what they said about adrenaline was true; the heaviness was all in her heart.

A hall away from the survival pod dock, she set down her children. She tapped the syncopated code on her temple, transmitting to Rachel through the microcommunicator grafted under her skin. She waited for a reply.

Nothing.

She began to sweat.

She shifted the laser rifle, swiveling it around, her fingers closing on its throttle. Her eyes darted about uncontrollably, the barrel of her weapon shaking, trying to follow them.

There was no one anywhere, and no sound but the faint, hollow clanking, more felt than heard, that meant spaceship instead of New York. No sound even from the dock, but she knew that Martin was there. Asleep, she hoped, but she wasn't going to count on it. It didn't really make a difference in the end.

At last, the tap-tock-tap-tock-tock sounded in her ear: the "okay" code from Rachel, so all was ready. Tiffany tapped a reply as she started methodically for the dock. Its door was open; Jan still had control of Medusa (of course she did, Tiffany thought, or they'd never have gotten this far).

Rachel's voice, a soft, seductive explosion, erupted in the silence:

"Hello, Martin."

A startled, male grunt. . . .

Tiffany pushed her weapon through the portal.

Rachel, draped in a diaphanous veil of thin, red satin, leaned against the side of the far entrance. A long leg ending in a black, spiked riser extended through the slit in her togalike garb. Martin's eyes never left her. She'd been an actress once, evoking calls of "Monroe!" and "Mercy!" from critics and vidfans alike. A few more vids and she might never have needed the comparisons, for all that was worth. She hadn't had the chance to accept more than one leading role.

Martin rose jauntily. Tiffany waited for him to clear the control panels, then she spun the throttle on the laser rifle, burning an inch-wide hole in his back. The heat sealed his arteries, and he hit the grating with a dull, bloodless smack.

The price of mortality, Tiffany thought grimly. She looked at Rachel: beautiful but deadly—like an old, trite, B-movie. Rachel stared emotionlessly at Martin's crumpled form as she waved her children into the dock from the corridor behind her. One, two, three—Mark, Marsha, and Diane. Jan's boy, David, tottered in behind them. Tiffany tossed her rifle to Rachel and went back for her twins.

Daniel hadn't moved, and Monica still slept. The boy watched Tiffany with that same, curiously complacent stare.

Tiffany thought he looked somehow older—older than he had when, a week before, they'd taken him and Monica and locked them in that motherless room.

What went on behind his eyes? She would never know. . . . At her belt, she fingered the memory cubes, one for Monica, two for Daniel. Thank God, she thought, that they'd had time to plan this. Each child had his or her own cube—Rachel's and Jan's wore theirs now on strings about their necks.

Painstaking, that task had been. In constant fear of discovery, Jan had disabled, then run a viral data download through Medusa's knowledge banks, collecting every conceivable education program along with the bulk of the data in the library subsystem's literary and aud banks. Together they'd spent countless nights tailoring the education systems and patching them into a modified copy of the survival pod control software. That in itself had been a torturous process; the pods had been designed for men, not children. At least the Sub-Space engineers had designed open-ended, malleable software. If they'd used a typical, closed architecture. . . . Tiffany didn't even want to think about it.

Tiffany looked into Daniel's eyes, realizing now how little time she'd had with him and his sister. She'd spent so much of herself just trying to ensure their futures: the programming, and the discussions—the arguments—with Jan and Rachel. They'd sabotaged the pods' abilities to transmit frequencies in the human vocal range. The children wouldn't even be able to talk to one another. Tiffany had argued against it, but Jan had won out in the end. Radio communications would be too dangerous; they had no idea who—or what—might overhear the children's conversations. For all they knew, killer satellites, ready to annihilate the source of any transmission in an unauthorized code, still lurked among the inner planetary orbits.

No, without radio, the pods would travel slowly—

silently—back to Earth. Like lifeless, insignificant, uninteresting chunks of rock. At least there *was* a way the children could talk, assuming they ever figured it out. Until then, they would be forced to learn, to *think*. With what Jan's program had stolen from the library, they would have books and music enough to last them centuries. And, after a few years, the pods would activate their existing, virtually comprehensive vidsystems, though Tiffany and her sisters had carefully censored out the heavily violent and sexual vid that passed as adult entertainment.

And even when Tiffany hadn't been working with Jan, when she'd still had the *chance* to spend time with her children, before things had finally come to a head with the family and they'd taken the children from them, she'd failed to relax, to be a doting mother, to be happy. She'd spent her time instead on pouring out her heart, her story, into the one large auxdata cube for Daniel. That had been another argument—Jan had built that cube from scratch, and she'd had time and materials for only one. It had gone, in the end, to the smartest child, Tiffany's son: Daniel, with his 189 IQ.

As Tiffany returned to the dock with Daniel and Monica, Rachel pushed Martin's body into the safety lock and ejected it out into the freezing void. The children stood around silently, watching them. Drugged, Tiffany finally realized. The bastards had drugged their children! She detached the large cube from her belt and hung it around Daniel's neck. It dug into her breasts as she lifted him, kissed him, then gave him over to the survival pod. She stepped in briefly to tap a command into the pod's keyboard, and a metallic voice broke the silence. "Command noted," the pod said. "Awaiting alternate opsystem load; insert override cube now."

Tiffany took Daniel's other cube from her belt and pushed

it into the pod's material interface. As she stepped out, she smiled again at Daniel. Almost immediately, the pod's hatch hissed closed. Before it sealed, she heard the pod's voice again. This time it was warmer, less harsh. "Hello, Daniel," it said. "I am your friend."

Tiffany began to cry; hurriedly, she lifted Monica, set her in her pod, and inserted her cube. She looked away then, taking the laser from Rachel and standing guard while her sister said her good-byes.

Jan's son, David, was last to go in. As Tiffany heard Rachel telling him that his mommy loved him but couldn't be there to kiss him, Tiffany signaled their status to Jan, then hurried to Martin's console seat and waited. After a moment, Rachel eased down onto the floor next to her.

Come on, Jan, Tiffany thought. It's all on you now.

"You've signaled?" Rachel whispered softly.

"Yeah."

"What will they do to us now?"

"Nothing. Jan's fixed the subspace drive—*they* couldn't do that. And without her to keep the drive running, they're helpless."

"But what if they won't let her take control? What if they just go crazy and kill her?"

"Then it won't matter. We'll all die, light-years from anything remotely resembling a planet." Tiffany looked over at the children in their survival pods. Daniel was crawling about on his cot, his hands pressing against the glassy smoothness of the pod's hull. "But our children will live."

"I'm scared, Tiff."

Tiffany said no more. She looked down, saw the tears welling in Rachel's eyes, and fought to hold back her own.

Deep within the *Falcon*, the subspace drive powered on; Tiffany felt the subtle, shifting vibrations in her feet. She straightened, then the receiver in her ear clicked several times. "Jan's ready," she said, spinning the console seat around, mashing a button that lowered a transparent blast-shield, sealing off the dock. Once the shield was in place, another button opened the main lock.

Against the starry black, the pods darkened, the tiny figures inside becoming shadows. Back to the womb, Tiffany thought. Alone this time—she wished they could ride together; maybe on a shorter journey, but the pods could handle only one adult each, and the children would grow. . . . Her hands started to shake; she clenched them together. She closed her eyes, then released the pods into the void. Rachel tapped out the next signal for Jan.

Tiffany held her breath, watching the spheres drift effortlessly away from the ship; they began to spin slowly, creating their weak, artificial gravity.

For a moment, she thought she saw Daniel looking back at her; then, one by one, the thrusters kicked in and the pods sped away into their programmed orbits.

Watching them disappear into starry pinpricks, Tiffany let herself breathe. That had been her last fear: that the pods' override cubes would somehow fail, damning the children to the *Falcon*'s starward trajectory, sending them out and away from the sun forever. Or almost forever, until the inertia wore away after a few thousand years and the sun's relentless gravity drew the spheres back into a fiery embrace.

Tiffany watched the pinpricks disappear, then Jan signaled her last ready signal, and Rachel closed the main lock, sealing the ship for its leap into subspace.

Daniel Tyler-Grant watched the silvery needle that had been his home until it suddenly blinked away into nothingness. Mommy? he thought, almost understanding. He looked

from his sphere at the others and wondered why they spar-
kled so against the black as they streaked along beside his
on their tails of white fire. After a while, his little hand
went to the thing hanging at his neck, and his sight focused
in on his new home.

Chapter

· 1 ·

"I AM DANIEL," he said. He was four and a half in Earth years, the only kind of years the sphere knew.

"Yes," the sphere said.

"I am human," he said.

"Yes," the sphere said.

"I am alone," he said.

"No. You have me. I teach you. I take care of you."

"But you're not like me. Not like the others. You're not human."

"No."

"And I am not with the others."

"Not yet."

"Then I am alone." Daniel paused, looking out at the cluster of spheres around his own. "Make me some paper."

A sound—a whir—came from the dark black box wedged between Daniel's bed and the desk Daniel could not yet sit at without the aid of two thick cushions. The edge of a clean, white sheet broke through the black surface. Daniel grasped at it and pulled the paper out. He sat at his desk and took up his pen, squinting out at the void. He began to draw.

"What are you doing, Daniel?" the sphere asked.

"Making pictures of stars."

"You should write."

Daniel ignored his teacher. "In that sphere there," he said, pointing out with his pen, "I see a face looking at me."

"That is your sister's sphere."

"Monica?" He was never sure himself because the sky spun around so much. His sphere had told him that if they didn't spin, he couldn't sit at his desk or sleep in bed. Once, Daniel had asked the sphere to stop spinning, and he'd floated all around the inside of the sphere. All his things had floated around, too, and it had taken him a long time to clean everything up.

"Yes," the sphere answered. "Monica."

"I want to talk to her."

"You cannot. My transmitters can broadcast only radar and pulsed emergency codes."

"What?"

"Nothing, Daniel. You cannot talk to your sister. Write."

"I don't want to write."

"Do you want to play a game?"

"No," he said simply.

"A cartoon? Cosmo-Mite and Zeke the Space-Hillbilly?"

"No."

Daniel sat at his desk, staring out at his sister's sphere. Hours passed. Daniel drew stars on the paper. He drew himself. He drew his sister. He wrote *Monica* on the paper. He wrote *Daniel*. He toyed with the big dark cube that the sphere refused to take from him, even though Daniel could remember his mother giving it a littler one. The sphere said the little cube told it what to teach him, but in that it was taking its time. About the big cube, the sphere would only say, "Not yet."

"Take this now?" Daniel asked, holding the cube up so that the sphere's eye—a glassy dome on top of the black box—could see it.

"Not yet."

Daniel fell silent and went back to his pictures. When the sphere spat out his tray with the protein cakes and the vitamin pellets, Daniel let it sit. He wasn't hungry, but he thought about *chicken* and *beans* and *bread* and *cow's milk* and the other words the sphere would list when it spoke about food. Daniel wondered what eating that sort of food could be like.

"You are sad?" the sphere asked.

"I feel like I did when you told me I was sad."

"Then you are sad. But you must eat."

Daniel shrugged and took up one of the protein cakes. He bit into it, still not understanding how it made any difference. But the sphere was his friend—his only friend, even if it wasn't human like him. Without the sphere, Daniel suspected he would die.

"You will talk to your sister one day," the sphere said.

"When?"

"I don't know. That knowledge does not reside in my higher centers."

"Where does it reside?"

"I don't know."

"Maybe it's in this," Daniel said, holding out the large cube again.

"Not yet," the sphere said.

"Why?"

"I don't know."

"Then why," Daniel insisted, "do I want to know things you can't tell me? Why do I want to know more than the others' names—Monica, Marsha, Mark, Diane, and David? That's all I know because it's all you will tell me."

"Tiffany Tyler-Grant—your mother's name. You know that."

"Yes, I know that. But what is *mother?* What is that?"

"Mother is she who gave you and your sister life. She gave birth to you."

"What is birth?"

"One day I will explain that. After you understand the words I need to use."

"Will *birth* let me understand my mother?"

"I don't know."

"Will it remind me of what she looked like? What she felt like?"

"You know what she looks like. You have seen the picture."

The picture, Daniel thought. Yes, he had seen it—so many times that he could close his eyes and see it as clearly as if it were on the console. He, also, was in the picture, standing next to Monica, both of them coming up to Tiffany's knee. Tiffany, Daniel knew, was beautiful. She had warm brown eyes, and she was always smiling. In the picture, everyone was smiling: Tiffany, Daniel, Monica, Mark, Marsha, Diane, David, David's mother, Jan, and especially the other lady, Tiffany's sister Rachel, with the bright red hair, the mother of the triplets that the sphere said meant that Mark, Marsha, and Diane had been born at the same time. Daniel and Monica were twins, which were like triplets except there were only two of them.

"Why can't you tell me more about the feelings?" Daniel asked impatiently. "And more about the others?"

"I only know their names, Daniel. I'm sorry."

Daniel held up the big cube again.

"Not yet."

"The sun looks bigger," Daniel said.

"Yes. So do you. You are growing."

Daniel sighed and went back to his pictures.

"Write," the sphere said.

Daniel wrote *I am Daniel* and *I am a boy* on the paper in the spaces between the stars. He showed it to the sphere's eye.

"Good," the sphere said. "You should exercise now, Daniel. You haven't in a long time."

Daniel looked into the sphere's eye, sighed, and moved to the flat platform at the foot of his bed. He sat down, lifted his knees to his chest a few times, closed his eyes, relaxed his body the way the sphere had taught him, then suddenly squeezed all his muscles tight. Relax, squeeze, relax, squeeze, relax, squeeze . . .

When he finished, Daniel got up and asked the sphere for a toilet tube. He used one, and he used the paper with the pictures he'd drawn and words he'd written to clean himself. His body felt sticky, so he asked the sphere for one of the wet, sweet-smelly, flimsy sheets of paper, and he cleaned himself all over. He felt cool and tingly, like he always did after his baths. Once, the sphere had told him that maybe one day he would take baths like other people in a tub full of steaming water or in a cool, clear lake. Daniel hadn't understood, so the sphere had shown him pictures on the libconsole. The sphere said some lakes were vast, full of millions of gallons of water, and that lakes were small compared to oceans.

Daniel still couldn't imagine that much water. He tossed the flimsy paper into the toilet tube, then he closed the tube and pushed it into the black box. The sphere hummed as it processed the toilet tube's contents. Daniel knew what it was doing because he had asked once what the sound was. The sphere called Daniel's toilet stuff "salvageable material." Daniel didn't care what it was as long as he didn't have to smell it.

"Why can't you teach me about my mother?" Daniel asked again.

"I cannot teach that. I can teach you language. I can teach you how to read and write and talk so that you can one day talk to your sister and the others. Later I can teach you math and physics and chemistry and biochemistry and many other things."

"What are they?"

"Things. You will not understand until you learn more language."

"Oh," Daniel said. He went back to a clean sheet of paper and drew more stars. After a while, he sighed and looked at the sphere's eye. "Okay," he said. "Teach me."

Chapter

·2·

■ *OUR SPHERES*, Daniel wrote, *are like planets except inside out. When I breathe on the glass, I make clouds.*

He stared at the words and gazed out at Monica's sphere. She, too, sat at her desk. . . . What did her sphere teach her? After a while, he crumpled up the paper and asked for a clean sheet. With sloppy strokes, he began to arrange the symbols the way the sphere had taught him, then he joined them with lines and showed the diagram to his teacher.

"Good, Daniel. You are learning very quickly."

He shrugged. "What use is making pictures of chemicals?" he asked. He was eight in Earth years, almost nine, and his education had bored him since the sphere had pronounced him linguistically competent. He worked only because if he didn't, the sphere wouldn't let him read. Yesterday he had read *Alice's Adventures in Wonderland, Candide,* and *The Hobbit.* Or part of *The Hobbit:* The sphere had blacked out the libscreen while Bilbo Baggins was hopelessly lost in a dark, slimy cave. Daniel had complained, but the sphere had told him he had to sleep. Daniel had asked it to tell him about caves, and it had told him some and shown him a few pictures on the console, but it still wouldn't let him find out what was going to happen to Bilbo. . . .

Right now, the console lit up with a black-and-white diagram, a mirror image of what Daniel had drawn on his paper. "That is the carbon-silicon compound that allows you life, Daniel. It is the composition of my hull, and it provides the energy that drives the photosynthesis cells that generate your oxygen. It traps the sunlight to do this, and this is also good. With nothing to trap the sunlight, you would burn."

"So? What good is this picture?"

"It is chemistry. It shows you how the parts of the universe fit together."

"Yes," Daniel said, almost automatically. He looked back at the paper and the figure he'd drawn. He looked out at his sister's sphere and the spheres of the others, then back at the paper. Under the diagram he'd drawn, he wrote *Glass Cages*, then put down his pen and stared meditatively back out.

The vector correction burners of the spheres were lighting—that meant asteroids. Daniel smiled; the near-misses were always exhilarating. It still scared him when the sphere failed to evade the little pieces, but he'd thought about it lately and decided the tinkling sound the asteroid dust made when it hit his sphere was like the sound of rain in the vid and the books.

Daniel squinted; the asteroids passed in formation—like a flock of birds—in front of the sun. "The cluster looks very dense," he said.

"Yes," the sphere replied.

Daniel continued to stare out. His hand went, as it often did, to the big memory cube at his neck. He still wore it almost all the time, even though it hurt him sometimes, its sharp corners bouncing against his naked chest. Absently and without looking, he held the cube up to the sphere's eye.

"Not yet," the sphere said.

Daniel sat back to watch the storm.

They came with a fury he'd never imagined. The spheres tried hard to enter tangentially. Somehow, they hadn't had enough time.

Daniel gripped the memory cube tightly and half-closed his eyes as his sphere nicked the edge of the first particle cloud. He began to smile, but his eyes opened wide, disbelievingly, as an adjacent sphere exploded.

Daniel screamed.

"Mark!" he cried. The sphere said nothing, and Daniel huddled down next to his bed and covered his head with his arms. The particles belted incessantly against the hull of the sphere; he thought over and over again of the diagram of the carbon-silicon compound, wishing it strength he knew it didn't possess. Mark's sphere was proof of that.

Daniel's sphere jerked violently, cracking his head against the desk. Still, he kept his eyes closed. Through the pain, he imagined the monstrous rocks whizzing past, imagined them smashing, grinding, devouring. . . . As he imagined these things, he cried.

The sphere said nothing until after it had cleared the cluster and turned off its burner. "You are sad?" it asked.

"Yes," Daniel answered.

"It is safe now, Daniel. Perhaps it will not happen again. We are nearing the orbit of Mars. Haven't you noticed the sun growing larger?"

"Yes," Daniel answered. "Mark's dead, isn't he?" he asked. He was still too afraid to look up.

"Yes. He is dead. Marsha is dying. The hull of her sphere cracked."

"Huh?" Daniel got up slowly and squinted out at Marsha's sphere. As he watched it, it spit several canisters toward each of the remaining spheres. "What's it doing?"

"She must be dead now. Her sphere is transferring its salvageable material before it shuts itself down."

"Shipping to us?" Daniel asked. He watched two of the canisters vector in on his sphere. They entered on the hull side of the black box.

"To us," the sphere said, "and to the others."

Daniel sat back at his desk and held his head in his hands. He thought about Mark and Marsha. They were brother and sister, just like he and Monica. Not anymore. "What happens when humans die?" he asked the sphere.

"Their biological unity breaks down into its component parts. The verb is decompose. I taught you that word."

"Yes," Daniel said. "But that wasn't what I was asking."

"It was what you asked. What did you mean to ask?"

"I—I don't know."

The hours passed; in despair Daniel returned to his routine tasks—his eating, his learning, his drawing. He felt numb, and it wasn't until he noticed the ache in his groin, until he realized he needed a toilet tube, that the idea came.

When it did, his heart fluttered; he could barely force out the words. "Those canisters," he whispered. "Can you send them to the other spheres?"

"Yes. If you perish, I am programmed to transfer salvageable material."

"Were those canisters from Marsha's sphere like the toilet tubes? They looked like them."

"They were toilet tubes."

Daniel laughed, feeling the skin of his face tighten under

its salty cake of dried tears. He grabbed up his pen and, on his paper, underneath the chemical diagram, he scribbled *I am Daniel. Hello!* He folded the paper and placed it inside one of the toilet tubes. He held it up to the sphere's eye.

"Send this tube to Monica's sphere," he said.

"Why?" the sphere asked. "It is a toilet tube."

"It's more than that now," Daniel said. "I have made it more than that. You *can* send it to her, can't you?"

"Yes. But I still don't understand. It is a toilet tube."

"If I rename it, will you understand? Can I call this a communication tube?"

"You can rename it. But you must define the term for me so that I can store it and respond to it in the proper manner."

"Okay," Daniel said excitedly. "A communication tube looks like a toilet tube, but it's used to send messages and things from one sphere to another."

"Stored. I understand your command now. Give me the tube."

Daniel hesitated, suddenly afraid that the absurdly simple idea would never work. Surely the sphere would have considered all possible ways of communicating with the other spheres . . . as many times as he'd asked?

His fear grew into terror as the thought of losing just this possibility of communication became more terrible than his previous resignation to no communication at all. Please, he thought, *please* . . .

Hesitantly, he shoved the tube into the black box. The sphere spat it out, and Daniel watched it vector toward Monica's sphere. His hands shook; he squeezed them into fists, then he watched Monica's sphere take in the tube.

She would have to think, Daniel realized. Her sphere would assume that he was dying. Had she even seen what he'd done? She had to think!

Please! he thought. He'd never felt emotion so strongly.

His whole life was changing. *Could be changing,* he corrected himself. *It has to work! It has to . . .*

Suddenly the tube shot back out of Monica's sphere, and Daniel laughed, then shouted for joy. He clenched his belly ecstatically as the tube homed in on his sphere.

"You are about to receive a communication tube," Daniel told the sphere. "When you receive communication tubes, you should pass them in to me."

"How will I know that it is not a salvageable material tube? If you call every tube a communication tube, I could pass in substances that would kill you."

"You will know if it is a salvageable material tube if another sphere is damaged."

"My programming tells me that I cannot always be sure if another sphere is damaged. One may be damaged, and I may not know."

Daniel frowned. "Okay," he said. "If you receive a tube that I have not told you to expect, you will tell me. I will look out and determine whether or not a sphere is damaged, and then I will tell you whether or not it is a communication tube."

"Now I understand," the sphere said, taking in the tube from the void. It handed it in through the black box to Daniel.

Daniel opened it excitedly. Inside was a piece of paper with a drawing of flowers and birds. Very beautiful, Daniel thought. She drew more nicely than he did. Underneath the picture, she had written, *Monica. Why couldn't we think of this before?* The ink at the end of her sentence was smeared. Daniel touched the paper—it felt wet. Monica had been crying. Why was she sad now? Daniel wondered. He wasn't sad. He wished he could understand.

He asked the sphere for more paper. He wrote messages for Diane and David, and the sphere sent them. Then Daniel wrote another for Monica. He drew a sad face, and underneath it he wrote, *Why are you so sad? We can talk! You should be happy!*

Daniel looked at the paper and smiled. He added, *Send more pictures. The flowers are beautiful!* Then he put the paper back into the tube and pushed it through the giving surface of the black box.

After shipping the tube, the sphere said, "You are growing, Daniel. You have passed a test. I will take the large memory cube now."

Hesitantly, Daniel fingered the cube, replaying the sphere's words in his mind.

"Give it to me," the sphere said.

Quickly, Daniel took off the strange necklace and pushed it into the black box. "What is it?"

"Aud-data; some vid, too. I am to play it at your request."

"Play it."

For the first time in years of memory, Daniel heard a voice other than his own or the sphere's. "Hello, Dan," the voice began, "I am Tiffany, your mother. You must be a strong young man now, and that is good. I'm sorry that I had to instruct your survival pod to wait so long before playing this for you, but you will see that it was necessary. I want so much for you to be able to understand. . . ."

The recording went on. It went on for days; Daniel interrupted it only to reply to messages from his sister and cousins. Already, the communication tubes flitted through space like flies, to and from the four surviving spheres.

Meanwhile, Daniel listened to his mother and gazed, fascinated at the pictures she showed him and talked about. At the end, he made the sphere start the recording over.

From the others, he learned that they did not have large cubes like his, and he'd learned from his mother that their spheres weren't equipped to play *his* cube. They wanted to know what Tiffany said. Daniel tried to explain, but his explanations just created more questions than he could begin to answer. In fact, he had countless questions of his own.

He tried to explain, but he failed, over and over again. Time passed, and he turned nine, and still he listened to the recording to the end and started it over. He stopped with his studies of math and chemistry; he was glad that the sphere let him.

More than once, Daniel tried to copy his mother's words onto paper for the others. But so many of the words were just for him, and in several places of the recording, she asked him to translate her story so that the others could understand. She said that he was the smartest, and that it was his task to understand her words, then to translate them so they would make sense in the environment in which he and and the others lived—for she could not comprehend his world of survival pods and isolation in the vast immensity of space.

When he heard her say that, Daniel was unsure whether he really comprehended their world of survival pods and space. He had so much to understand.

Chapter

·3·

Alone, weightless
Like a message in a bottle
My tears would be rain
But rain falls on Earth
Seeps into soil
Seeks out the roots of life, green
My tears only dry,
Smears on the sphere
Which I clean and cry again

■ DANIEL READ THE POEM until he knew it by heart, then he told the sphere to remember it, and he read it a final time aloud. It was David's, and tear-stained; it had passed through Diane and Monica before it had reached Daniel.

David was always lonely, and he was always writing poems that were this sad or sadder. He wrote poems about the blackness of space. He wrote poems about Earth, about the books he read, about the vid he watched. The poems were often sad, even when the books or vid were happy. Only when David wrote poems about Monica's pictures were they happy; Daniel suspected that David wrote the happy ones out of fear. He was afraid Monica would be mad at him and not send him pictures if he wrote sad things about them.

Daniel and the girls tried to comfort David, but it seldom seemed to do much good. Ironically, halfway through Daniel's tenth year, David had told them that his sphere had lost its vector correction thrusters. Should they ever need to change course, David would be left behind.

After Daniel had learned this, he'd begun to memorize David's poems and, also, say them to his sphere so the sphere would know them, too. He hadn't told the others about this practice; he saw no point in making them depressed. But he did it because, if David died, he and the girls would want his poetry to remember him with. They had nothing but the picture with which to remember Mark and Marsha. . . .

Diane, more than any of them, threw herself into her studies. Daniel felt sorry for her; once she had been a triplet, but now she was like David: no real sisters or brothers. In a way, she had adopted David. She'd taken the task of David's salvation as her own, and she would propose long, technical plans for the twins, far beyond their abilities to comprehend. Beyond, as well, the understanding of the survial pods' computers, a fact that frustrated Diane because, *if* they could understand, they could make the parts David's sphere needed to build a new vector correction system. But David's sphere couldn't understand even how to do that.

On the practical side, Diane had informed them that the spheres were on an intercept orbit with Earth, and she'd calculated the exact number of years, days, hours, and minutes it would take them. As Daniel read David's poem, he knew that they would reach Earth in five Earth years and fifty-three days. He didn't know how many hours and minutes, but he knew that, if he asked Diane, she could tell him.

Now Daniel was eleven in Earth years. The spheres had cleared the asteroid danger zone and were inside the orbit of Mars. With luck, David wouldn't need his vector correction system until Earthfall.

Daniel had spent most of the past two years listening to his mother's words, reading everything that seemed even remotely interesting in the sphere's lib catalogue, and devouring the sphere's endless collection of vid. Sometimes when he thought of his mother's words, he thought of some of the vid, especially things like *Road Warrior,* because the people looked so much like those his mother described. But there, the resemblance ended. Stigg, Monk, Karmen, and the others—all those of whom Tiffany spoke—they were like children; they were like *Peter Pan* or *Alice's Adventures in Wonderland,* sometimes even like the legendary rock band Spinal Tap, who were, Daniel thought, like children anyway. Many times, Daniel had thought simply, they were like us.

Long before, Daniel had given up trying to describe Tiffany's story to the others. That day, just before he'd received David's latest poem, he'd decided to tell the story from the inside out so the others would see the natures of the people who had formed the worlds of those women who had given them birth. And he'd decided, finally, that he was ready.

* * *

With Monica, Daniel communicated most, and his desire to help her understand, more than anything else, forced his pen to paper the way it did. They would often write to each other of the beauty of the things they would see on Earth, and Daniel was forever amazed at how Monica could breathe life into her drawings of things that he could only picture as flat things inside the vid-screen.

Once, Monica had sent Daniel a picture of herself that she'd drawn from a mirrored reflection in the hull of her sphere. Daniel had decided that she was more beautiful than any of the other things she drew, even more beautiful than Tiffany or Rachel or any of the heroines in the vid. He'd tried for several days to draw himself, but he'd only gotten frustrated, even though he'd eventually sent the best of the end results to Monica anyway. She'd written that it was nice, but Daniel knew better.

Daniel thought of all these things as he sat down to write. He couldn't write poetry like David, and he couldn't begin to try to save David like Diane could. And he couldn't draw like Monica. All he had was Tiffany's story and her desire that he tell the others. That, by his mother's wish, had become his life.

At the top of a clean sheet of paper, Daniel wrote *How We Came Here*. He stared at the words. After *Here* his pen had suddenly stopped. Time passed, and Daniel frowned at his title. He asked the sphere for another clean sheet, and, at the top, he wrote, simply, *Earth*.

Thusly, he began. Frustration came and went, and, on some days, he could write nothing at all. When it worked, he would read his writing aloud to the sphere and then argue endlessly about grammar and spelling and the meanings of words. But he did write; he was eleven and a half before he sent out the first part for the others to read. . . .

·EARTH·

PART ONE

I.

Stigg blew away the dirt from the wood and traced the ancient lettering with one black, jagged fingernail. Putting down his magic candle, he flexed his thick muscles and pulled the box screaming and scraping over the rubble and into the light. Big, he thought. He tapped the box. He lifted the near end; it came up easily. Not too big, he thought.

Running his rough tongue over the back of his crooked teeth, he grinned. He took the metal bar from the toolkit at his belt and shoved its point into the crack under the box's lid, prying it open, aiming his magic candle inside. The black metal rat-tats shone dully under the light. Stigg dug through them, and he smiled again when his fingers found the boom-balls. He counted fifteen of them. He lifted one out and traced its rough surface thoughtfully. He stuck one fingernail into the little metal ring and yanked it away. He stepped away from the box, then he held the boom-ball up to his ear.

"Boom!" the ball said to Stigg. Its voice reverberated hollowly through the dark passages.

"Boom!" Stigg exclaimed back to his empty hand. He stood there, letting the rocks bounce off his head and shoulders before scraping the boom-ball's little metal shards from his palm. He searched his ear and the side of his head, feeling for more little bits of metal. He found a few; they fell out when he touched them. He laughed. "Boom!" he repeated.

Stigg put the lid back on the box and hammered it shut. He shone his magic candle into the space from which he'd pulled the box, looking for more. When he found none, he grumbled, then he bent to pick up the box itself.

Stigg carried it back through his passages. He stopped at his home and added three of the boom-balls to his private collection, arranging them on his pretty shelf around the glass frog that Henna had traded him for a box of firewater. That was so long ago that Stigg could barely remember anything from that time except the trade. He'd been stupid then—he hadn't known you could drink the firewater and feel it racing all around inside. He'd learned that from Henna only after the trade, and he'd felt cheated. But, still, he liked the little frog—it reminded Stigg of Stigg. Tough, Stigg thought. Stigg is tough!

And Stigg had found plenty of firewater since the trade to make up for it. And Algy was always ready to trade him the firewater that he made for the rat-tats and boom-balls and other things that Stigg found in the passages around his home.

Stigg sat down on his wooden pallet and looked at the arrangement on his pretty shelf. He saw some dirt on the frog and frowned; he picked it up, blew off the dirt, and set it back.

From above, he heard smashing sounds: Fiberglass Muskrat getting some daylight practice. Stigg decided to listen for a while before taking the box up to Algy. While he listened, he thoughtfully drank two bottles of the white firewater Algy called gin; then he sighed, deciding he'd better go before Algy left his lab for the Batcave and Muskrat's *real* show.

Stigg hated the daylight, which was why he lived where he lived while all the others either slept in the open or in caves or in houses they'd had Algy design for them. It was hard to persuade Algy to spend his time on such things. Algy preferred to study the things Stigg and the others brought him—he preferred to make his own firewater, and he really liked making the old machines work. Stigg remembered the day Algy had actually made sound come out of the strange music boxes and how everybody had gone wild that night and drank more firewater than Stigg had previously imagined possible. And Stigg remembered the later day when Algy had made the guitars and the other music machines work. That was when Monk, Karmen, the Stick, and the others had gone wild. Nobody had known they would become the great Fiberglass Muskrat. Nobody except them, Stigg supposed. And now just about everybody preferred to see Muskrat live to watching the picture machines of the old bands that Algy had also made work. When Stigg found the picture tapes and disks, he didn't even try to take them to anyone but Algy or Monk anymore. Monk wanted them for ideas, he'd told Stigg. Everyone else just wanted Muskrat, and Algy was now working on making things to capture Muskrat's music like the ancients had done with their bands.

Stigg had thought of trading Algy some things to make him a house so he could live on the surface, but when Stigg thought about that he felt uncomfortable. Stigg had *always* lived in his passages. The passages were all he knew, and if he left, Stigg feared he would just feel more stupid than he usually did. And when he thought about this, he realized that he'd rather just have Algy make his machines work because it was only Fiberglass Muskrat and the Batcave that made Stigg want to be on the surface at all. Before Muskrat's first show, he'd gone up only to trade, or maybe for one of the women if he'd been feeling really lonely. Now, he went to the Batcave every night.

Stigg picked up his box and stumbled with it through his passages. The turnings had begun to confuse even him; that was why he'd started a map to carry with his tools so he couldn't get lost in his growing home. Since he'd learned to use the boom-balls to blow away walls separating one passage from another, he'd made his maze very large indeed. One day, he thought, he would bring Monk down to show him all the wonders he had found! Maybe he could even make a room big enough to be his own Batcave, then he could invite everybody into his home!

But, with the box balanced on his back, Stigg couldn't look at his map. He had to crease his forehead, making his brain *remember*. Sometimes that hurt.

By the time Stigg made it up, Muskrat had finished its practice, and the music coming from the Batcave was some of the old stuff—Prince or Jimi Hendrix, Stigg wasn't sure which. On the picture machines, they looked a lot alike: dark, like Monk and Nightshade. And Stigg, whenever he spent long times in the daylight.

He hurried to the white brick building Algy had built for his lab. Stumbling through the big door, Stigg almost collided with Monk's back. He caught himself just in time. He watched Monk's feet turn and point at him.

"You found a big one this time, my friend," Monk said kindly.

"Stigg is tough!" Stigg tried to look up at Monk, but he could see only as high as Monk's belt. If he stood, he would fall back and smash the box all over Algy's floor.

"Stigg will break Stigg's back one day carrying things like that whether Stigg is tough or not," Algy said from somewhere behind Monk. "Take it from him, Monk, and put it down somewhere."

Stigg straightened his back as the weight was lifted. He smiled up at Monk as the big man carried the box to one of Algy's work tables. "Monk is tougher than Stigg," Algy pointed out.

Stigg nodded. Monk was very smooth, much smoother than Stigg, but Stigg *knew* that Monk was tough. Once, he had seen Monk hold ten boom-balls in his big hands and make them all boom at once. Even Stigg was afraid to do that many boom-balls at one time. But after the booms had stopped, Monk had just smiled.

Stigg watched Algy hobble over to the box and brush at the markings on its side. Stigg thought that Algy could be tough like him if only he would spend some time smashing rocks with Stigg in his home and listening to boom-balls, but Algy always laughed at Stigg's suggestions. Still, Stigg liked Algy, even more than most of the others, because Algy was smart. Algy, for instance, could read. "What does it read?" Stigg asked.

"M-60, twenty each. M-301, ten each. Fifteen grenades. And it says, *'Handle with care.'* "

"Huh?"

Algy looked up at Stigg and smiled. "Rat-tats and boom-balls."

"That's what's in the box!" Stigg exclaimed.

"Yes," Algy said with a laugh. He opened the box,

pulled out an M-60, and tossed it to Monk. Monk caught the gun and tested its weight.

"These really were weapons, weren't they?" Monk asked Algy.

Algy looked at him, curiously cocking one frayed, bushy eyebrow. "Yes."

"They actually killed people?"

"Yes. You've seen the old picture stories. Strange world it must have been, eh?" Algy picked out the grenades and set them beside the box. "Why don't you take these and go blow up some rocks somewhere before the show? Take the rest of the band. Get some energy up."

Monk put down the M-60 and caught the grenades as Algy tossed them to him one by one. He grinned at Stigg on the way out. "Thanks for the boom-balls, Stigg. Be there tonight?"

"Always. Stigg is always at the Batcave when Muskrat plays!"

"Of course." Monk laughed and left.

"Well, Stigg," Algy said. "Half a case of gin?"

"Whole case! Algy always gives Stigg a *whole* case!"

"Yes, I know, but I have enough of these," Algy said, hefting one of the submachine guns. "They're interesting toys, but the others are getting tired of playing with them. Have you heard many rat-tats lately?"

Stigg thought a moment. "No?"

"No. Okay, Stigg, I'll give you a whole case this time. But don't bring me any more rat-tats. Mark them on your map, though, so you can find them later if we need the metal."

"Boom-balls?"

Algy laughed. "Use them yourself, or bring them up. It doesn't matter. They're always fun."

Stigg nodded, then waited impatiently for Algy to get him his case of firewater. Algy brought it out of one of his

many rooms, thanked Stigg, and Stigg started back for his
home.

II.

Stigg drank one of his new bottles of firewater and listened
to Muskrat play with his boom-balls. The sound came more
from his passages than from above, and Stigg hoped that
Monk wasn't caving in the corridor to his secret underground
river. The booms came from that direction. Stigg looked at
the three boom-balls he'd kept and shrugged. He could
always make more passages.

He relaxed and drank. As long as Muskrat was tossing
around the boom-balls, it couldn't possibly be setting up to
play. This way, Stigg had time.

When the booms stopped, Stigg decided to stay on his
pallet and drink another bottle of firewater and wait until
Muskrat started to tune up. Monk always wanted to practice
a few new songs before opening the Batcave's doors anyway. And three bottles isn't enough, Stigg thought. Four
would put Stigg in the mood. He grinned at his wisdom,
belched, and winked at his frog.

When he heard the pat-patting in his passages, Stigg
nearly dropped his bottle. He wondered who could be coming to see *him*. He got excited—visitors never came into
Stigg's home unless he enticed them with six or eight bottles
of firewater. Only once had Stigg had a woman in his home,
and she, Henna, had been very, very drunk that night.

Stigg turned off his magic candle, deciding to surprise
his visitor. Stigg couldn't see much without light, but
unless his visitor had a magic candle, Stigg would see better.
After his eyes got used to the darkness, Stigg decided that
his visitor didn't have a magic candle. The pat-pats were

very close now, and Stigg still saw no light. When the pat-patting reached the passage beside the alcove where Stigg kept his cot, his pretty shelf, and his other things, he grinned and clicked on his magic candle.

"'Sprise!" Stigg exclaimed.

Across from him stood a pale, thin girl. Her hair was tangled, matted, and very long, longer than she was. She was very dirty, but underneath the dirt she was naked. Even with all the dirt, Stigg could tell that she was smooth—smoother even than Monk, Henna, Jack the Weasel, or Nightshade—much smoother than Stigg or Algy or most of the others. She stood motionlessly before him, staring at his magic candle. Stigg tried to remember if he had seen her before, then decided that he had not.

"'Sprise?" Stigg tried again. The girl didn't blink, didn't move.

"Hello?" Stigg tried. No answer.

Slowly, Stigg crept out of his alcove to the girl. He passed his hands in front of her eyes. She kept staring into the light. He touched her; she didn't react. But when he nudged her toward his alcove, she moved. He guided her to his pallet.

At first, he tried to clean her off by blowing on her the way he did the frog, but under her dirt was something wet and sticky. Stigg poured a little firewater onto one of her shoulders and rubbed. The dirt came off that way. He clicked his fingers in front of her eyes—he wanted to try one last time to talk to her before wasting the firewater on cleaning her. She might not want to be cleaned. But still, she didn't respond, so he dumped the bottle over her head.

After soaking the girl with firewater, Stigg rubbed the dirt from her body. He didn't feel very comfortable when he rubbed off her breasts and thighs, and he tried to get through those parts as quickly as possible. When Stigg did that to a girl, she was supposed to do one of two things:

She was supposed to tell him to stop, or she was supposed to moan and gasp and make other exciting sounds. Sometimes a girl would do both of those things at the same time. This girl did none of that; she just sat there, staring at his magic candle.

Finally, Stigg got her clean, drying her with one of the towels that Henna had given him. Then he sat here, looking at her. He'd run out of things to do.

From above, the sounds of Fiberglass Muskrat began to filter down through the rock. Stigg jumped with the first gut-wrenching chord of "Wrath of the Mole King," then he settled back to listen from where he was and figure out what to do with the girl. Stigg, he thought, solved first problems first. He opened a fresh bottle of firewater, drained it in one very long gulp, and opened yet another.

He drank half of the new bottle before thinking of trying it on the girl. With one hand, Stigg held back her head and forced open her mouth. With the other, he poured the firewater down her throat.

Almost immediately, she coughed and gagged, and her whole body began to shake. Stigg grew suddenly afraid. He'd never seen anyone die before, but this was what he'd always imagined dying might look like. He grabbed the girl and started to shake her.

"Don't die!" Stigg exclaimed. "Don't die!"

Suddenly her eyes opened wide and Stigg realized that she saw him and not the magic candle. She jerked violently away, bouncing back on the pallet and tangling herself in her hair, then she screamed, and her hand went to her bottom. When she brought her hand back through her mass of hair, her fingers were bloody.

The pallet bit her! Stigg thought, amazed. "You *are* smooth!" he said.

She looked desperately from her hand to him and back down to her naked body. She backed farther away from him on the pallet, this time more carefully. She said something to Stigg that Stigg didn't understand.

"Stigg doesn't understand," he said slowly. "Are you scared?" he asked. "Don't be scared. Stigg won't hurt you."

She looked at him fearfully and again said the words that Stigg didn't understand.

Stigg scratched his chin, then hesitantly held out his bottle of firewater to the girl, motioning for her to drink. She took it, sniffed it, and put it to her lips. She swallowed and choked again. But just when Stigg thought it was going to make her die, she took another drink. When she stopped, she wiped her mouth with the back of her hand and handed the bottle back to Stigg. Stigg smiled. He finished the bottle and opened another.

The girl reached out for the towel with which Stigg had dried her. Stigg watched her closely. Noticing his curiosity, she made wrapping motions around her body. Stigg raised an eyebrow, then he went to the place behind his pallet where he kept those parts of his collection that didn't fit nicely on his pretty shelf, and he picked out the old robe that Henna had forgotten to take with her that time she'd come there. Stigg offered the robe to the girl. She took it and frowned at it, but she put it on after carefully pulling the sharp bit of wood from her behind. Stigg shivered—he didn't like the sight of so much blood. He handed the new bottle to the girl and opened himself another.

Stigg picked up the little glass frog from from his pretty shelf and handed it to the girl. She took it, turned it over in her hand, and smiled at Stigg.

"Pretty," Stigg said. "You are pretty, too," he added.

"Pretty?" the girl repeated after him, pointing at the frog.

"Uh—no, that is frog," Stigg said slowly. "That is pretty frog."

"Pretty frog? Pretty frog," she said, and she smiled again.

Stigg smiled back. He pointed at himself. "Stigg," he said.

"Stigg," the girl said. She pointed at herself. "Tiffany," she said.

"Tiffany," Stigg repeated. "Pretty Tiffany."

The girl looked confusedly from Stigg to the frog. "Pretty?" she asked.

Stigg nodded, he took the frog back from her, ran his hand softly over it, and said, "Pretty frog, pretty Tiffany." When Stigg smiled again at Tiffany, she backed away from him again and looked scared. Stigg set the frog carefully back on his pretty shelf, then he opened his hands and held them up. "Stigg thinks Stigg knows what Tiffany is thinking. Tiffany shouldn't think that. Stigg civilized!"

Her expression didn't change much. Stigg shrugged, tipped his bottle, and decided he'd better let Algy figure out how to talk to the girl before he said something to make her run away or maybe even die. Stigg had never known anyone so smooth, and he wasn't sure how much it would take for her to die. When Muskrat launched into "Home Is Where My Bottles Are," Stigg began to sway with the music. He smiled when he noticed that the girl's foot was tapping in time.

"Fiberglass Muskrat!" Stigg told her happily. He made motions with his hands like Karmen did when she played her guitar.

Tiffany actually laughed. She mimicked Stigg and began to make guitar sounds with her mouth. Fuzzy sounds, Stigg thought; then he, too, began to laugh. He made walking signs to the girl with his fingers, touched his ear, then made the guitar motions again. He raised an eyebrow.

The girl nodded and shrugged, fidgeting with the ragged claws on the ends of her fingers as if they bothered her. And she grabbed her hair and frowned. She looked up at Stigg, making clipping motions on her hair like she wanted to cut it off. Stigg nodded at her and gave her a sharp knife from his toolkit. She took it, frowned again, but she used it to shear off her hair so that it only came halfway down her back instead of all the way to her feet and then some.

While Tiffany cut her hair, Stigg laughed again, tipped his bottle back, and drained it. He looked at her, expecting to see her bottle empty as well, but it was still almost full. She handed back the knife and stared at him dumbly.

Stigg motioned for her to finish her bottle, and her eyes grew wider still. She shook her head, placed one hand over her stomach, and made a sick face. She really was smooth, Stigg reminded himself. He took back the bottle, finishing it himself rather than capping it, tossed the empties aside, and picked up his magic candle. He shook his head, smiled unsurely at the girl, then motioned for her to follow him off into his passages.

III.

Beneath fifty feet of bedrock, the hiss of hydraulic pumps broke the dark silence as they forced more oxygen into the waking sleeper's module.

When the pumps stopped, a hollow, faint whooshing took over. It was a muffled, distant-seeming sound, though, in truth, its source was a breach in the adjacent chamber. The complex's main computer stepped up its processing, engaged external life-support systems, and switched on the neon banks in all primary-use areas as well as in the waker's chamber. As the invading oxygen whisked away the last wisps of the cryogenic gas, the white light fell on the man's features. Under his head, his dark hair lay tangled and matted, foaming up on either side, the whole mass resembling a pillow. His mustache completely covered his mouth before blending into a soft, peaceful-looking beard that reached to his solar plexus. Below the point of the beard, his hands rested, curled slightly, moved over the years by the long, convoluted things that no longer resembled fingernails. He was naked, and similar growths graced the tips of his toes.

Tubes running to needles attached to each arm connected him intravenously to his module's computer. The main computer instructed the module to suck out the last of the cryonutrient solution that had sustained the man over the millennia. That done, the module filled the vacuum in the tubes with a carefully formulated solution of adrenaline, advanced counterhypnotics, and the man's own blood.

After a moment, the index finger of the man's right hand twitched.

The main computer took control of the module and regulated the revival procedure. Much had to be done properly and, though the module had been designed for the job, its designers had felt it wiser to place as much control as possible in the processors of the eighth-generation mainframe. If problems were encountered, Medusa alone had the intelligence to solve them.

Slowly, the man wakened. As his eyes fluttered open, the computer dimmed the lights and opened the bubble of the module.

The man began to sit, then bolted into that position as his disused muscles spasmed. He gripped his stomach, heedless of his claws. He heaved—dry. His tear ducts kicked in, and tears streamed down his cheeks. He was aware, barely, of his chamber door hissing open, and the droid that rolled in. It carried a tray bearing a glass of liquid, as much medicine as nutrient, and he reached for it with all the desperation of a man dying of thirst grasping at misty raindrops. It was like moving through fire, and his clacking fingernails bent and broke, nearly spilling the glass. But he made it.

He drank, gagged, sputtered up the first bit, then forced

down more. Even after that, it was long before his body reached equilibrium and he dared to climb out of the module. By then his droid had brought him a robe and clippers and shears for his nails and beard.

As he stepped down to the floor, his nose finally woke, and a sweet-sour odor filled his nostrils. Me, he thought. *Shower*.

"Good morning, Mr. Philip," the computer's sultry feminine voice piped sweetly. "I trust you slept well?"

He tried to grunt, then cleared his throat. *God, the taste!* "Morning?" he managed, testing his voice, then, "What year?"

"Sixty forty-nine."

Long time, he thought. He shook his head, regretting it for the sharp pains that speared up his neck. But it worked; his thoughts gained coherence, began to clear. *6049*. "That's nearly two thousand goddamn years too early!"

"Correction. Two thousand years earlier than planned."

He coughed. "Please, Medusa. You know what I meant."

"True," replied the computer in her even, seductive tones. "Why?"

"System malfunction. The outer wall has been breached by an unknown violent impact. I have sealed the chamber in question. I now require human direction as per my programming."

He imagined sarcastic undertones in the computer's voice. No, he thought, they'd been there; he'd actually heard them. Damn thing probably thought it could handle the problem alone. With his luck, it probably could. . . .

"Where?" he asked.

"To your left."

He glanced. "My sister?"

"Tiffany Tyler-Grant. Your sister, yes."

He took a step, then yelped, hopped, made the problem worse, and finally landed jarringly on his rear end. He touched the bloody balls of his feet, gingerly easing the broken bits of toenail from his flesh. Twisting around, he fumbled again for his clippers. "Thanks, Medusa," he said.

"For what?"

"Reminding me to clip my toenails."

"But I didn't do that."

He started to reply but chuckled instead. In four thousand years, his rapport with that machine still hadn't improved! He sighed, finished the task at hand, and rose carefully. He turned to the droid and indicated the pile of nails. It rolled over them, sweeping them up.

"How is she, Medusa?"

"Your sister? I don't know. I lost local sensors during the impact."

He went to the door and touched it, feeling for extreme temperature variations. The computer second-guessed him. "Normal Earth climate, Mr. Philip. Surface temperature, twenty-four degrees Celsius. Atmosphere has increased in nitrogen and carbon-dioxide concentrations, but oxygen level remains well above the acceptable minimums. Surface radiation has hovered just above preholocaust levels for the past two millennia. Date is April 17. Sunny skies, no rain since last week. No local tectonic activity. Minor seismic activity, however, has increased a hundredfold over the past century."

"The cause of the damage?"

"That is a possibility."

He grunted. "Open the door."

Without vocal response, the computer activated the portal. Philip peered into darkness; the light from his own chamber showed a thickness in the air—light dust that swirled lazily in the changing air currents.

"Try the lights, Medusa," he said, and they switched on almost immediately.

The chamber, identical to his except that it had but one

access, sported a gaping, two-foot hole in the far wall. His eyes fell darkly on the only important feature, the cryogenic module. Its bubble lay open, like his. Open, and empty. "She's gone," he said. He stepped into the room, quickly verified that the module was empty, peered briefly into the darkness beyond the the breach, then exited, ordering Medusa to reseal the portal again.

Rubbing his head, he slid down the wall of his chamber and sat on the floor. Gone, he thought, trying to organize his thinking for this unexpected turn of events. Gone. And that was no "minor seismic activity" that had made that hole. That was an explosion, and he had to assume a deliberate one. Things didn't spontaneously blast through elastic polymers and a foot of twenty-first-century, designed-to-last-forever concrete just for the hell of it. Not even explosives—they had to be placed. And that was a tunnel he'd peered into. Wasn't there before. . . .

He had to think of what to do!

Shower first. Try to eat something. . . .

An hour later, he sat in the command center of Tyler-Grant Complex Two, feeling the full weight of his thirty-two years (plus several thousand more, he imagined, though the human aging process was effectively nullified by the Hansel-Stutzman-Tyler-Grant cryogenic process). Hunched over thoughtfully in the swivel chair before Medusa's master control console, he resisted a sudden urge to wake the rest of the family. It was his duty, his task, to handle this as best he could. Alone. If he woke the others, he'd be committing them to a life in a still mostly desolate, certainly barbaric world. And worse, if he alerted Complex One without a very good reason, Mother Grant would have his balls for her first breakfast.

He'd already sent a drone back into Tiffany's chamber

and through the breach. He'd learned through infrared inspection that several shafts wended up to the surface there, though their paths were too convoluted to carry light to the tunnel's depths. The tunnel itself ran lengthwise, parallel to the north wall of the complex. It touched only at that one place—at the breach. The floor was strewn with rubble, much too uneven to allow the droid passage. If he could trust the infrared readings he'd obtained, he had evidence of the recent passing of only one warm-blooded being. The footprint pattern was erratic—it could belong to Tiffany, or something laboring under her weight. No way of knowing for sure.

Droid inspection of the surface had revealed several long cracks in the bedrock above the area of the breach. Footprints of varying detail covered what bits of soft ground the droid could find. Humanoid footprints, but disturbingly not quite human. Some toes were in the wrong place, some were missing, some seemed normal except for sharp, half-inch depressions at the tip of each toe. And all over the area—ragged pockets in the bedrock, shards of metal . . . grenade pins. There was even an abandoned, clean, M-16E machine gun.

No blood that he could find. No bodies.

Creatures out there? Yes, he thought. Creatures made a tunnel? Probably not. It was probably a tunnel used for access during the complex's construction that had failed to seal. Or it had sealed but been cleared later by—something.

So—had the creatures, whatever they were, purposefully blown a hole into Tiffany's chamber? Probably not. There was only that one set of prints, and, erratic as the prints were, they seemed to begin inside the chamber. But . . .

Philip sent another droid into Tiffany's chamber. He followed its progress out into the tunnel, and through its eyes, the images it saw displayed on one of Medusa's many CRT's.

Yes, the floor by the breach did perceptibly rise up to the main corridor. "Send it in as far as it will go, Medusa. Scan the floor with a magnification factor of ten."

The picture on the CRT showed that the computer complied. It didn't take long. "Stop," he said.

He would have smiled at his ingenuity had it evinced itself under other circumstances. There they were, big as life: dusty, ragged scraps of toenails.

He couldn't believe the implausible theory it all led up to. Someone or something had engaged in warfare, weapons practice, or something on the surface, and a high-impact grenade or other live projectile—or projectiles—had fallen through one of the rifts in the bedrock, reached the tunnel, rolled down to the nearest low point—by Tiffany's wall—and exploded. Just perfectly enough to break all the way through. Just neatly enough to disrupt Medusa's peripheral surveillance systems in the chamber. Just conveniently enough to wake him up centuries before his allotted time. . . .

Leaving him a problem to solve.

Tiffany was obviously alive—she'd walked out of the chamber. Her module must have initiated emergency revival procedures when it lost contact with Medusa and detected what it must have perceived as a radical shift in environment.

God only knew what state of mind Tiffany was in. Physically active, yes. But mentally competent? Would a mentally competent woman squeeze through a hole in the darkness to wander off wherever it might lead her?

No.

"Medusa, without your help, and given the data we have at hand, what are the chances that my sister still lives?"

"Impossible to evaluate. She was physically intact when she left. Probably operating at an extremely low degree of conscious awareness. Otherwise, all data would suggest paralysis by fear."

"You mean, I would have found her trembling in a corner?"

"Yes."

That made sense, he thought—just what he'd been thinking. Even Tiffany, awake, confronted by total darkness and actually remembering her past enough to imagine what had happened, would be gripped by terror. Even if she couldn't raise Medusa, she would never be irrational enough to leave.

And who knew what she'd encountered out there?

And so Philip reflected. Even if Tiffany was dead, he couldn't ignore that hole. He couldn't ignore the tunnel. Where there was a tunnel, there was a reason for it. If something had cleared it, then that something probably used it. And if that something had discovered a hole leading into what was obviously not a natural cavern . . . and a doorway (no less), promising more of the same . . .

He could always cave in the tunnel. But that was no guarantee that it wouldn't be excavated again. . . .

And then Tiff was still out there. Somewhere.

"Shit!"

He considered options. In the end, he saw only two: wake the complex's militia, or seek out Tiffany by himself.

The first option was irrevocable. Though Medusa could return a small number, himself included, to their centuries-long sleep, large numbers would tax her resources beyond her capacity. And though the present situation was potentially disastrous—for instance, Philip had to defeat the tunnel problem once and for all—the family could well need its military strength after two thousand more years of hibernation.

Mother Grant and her brother had carefully planned for emergence into a blossoming Earth—one in which mankind had again risen above savagery, one in which the family could again prosper and maintain its wealth among societies diverse enough to offer the creature comforts to which the Grant clan was accustomed.

They had taken technology underground with them— equipment and knowledge designed to carve them an invincible niche in the future. But invincibility could be fleeting. The Grants did not want to be autonomous in a world unto themselves; they wanted to fit in, possibly to rule, and that desire would be in great peril should the future decide it only wanted to take from them. Their military strength would discourage such ambition on the part of whatever petty warlords they might encounter, and, in addition to its militia, Complex One had quite an impressive array of military armament, including a few nuclear warheads. . . .

But it was Philip's responsibility to take care of eventualities such as this. If he wasted or abused resources, it would not bode well for him should Mother Grant decide he had acted in haste.

"Medusa!"

"Yes, Mr. Philip."

"Prepare the battle droid. I want to scout farther afield."

IV.

Seventeen miles south of Complex One, Complex Two was just over one mile northwest of the Batcave and the few other real structures that comprised the mutant community. Fifteen miles west of that, and hooking around to the north to form a geological cradle, an ancient, weather-worn mountain range loomed, its rounded peaks harboring the several lakes that fed water to the valley through rivers and streams both over- and underground. These waterways all spilled into the Atlantic or the flooded lower Hudson delta within thirty-five miles of the Batcave.

Most of the mutants lived in the community founded years before by the wise one called Algy and the ebon giant, Monk of the Fiberglass Muskrat. Despite their years, most in this odd society had little recollection of years past; it was as if Nature had taken pity on them and stripped away the long-term memory capacities of their ancestors. This, of course, was not true in all cases.

One of the wiser ones, one who could usually *remember,* went by the name of Bobo. He lived away from the central encampment in a warm, dry cave in the foothills of the mountains. For Algy and Monk, he was their sentinel in the west. Over the years, few had crossed the mountains in either direction. Those who had left had never returned; those who had come had seldom been friendly. But, to date, none but the last wave of invaders—the terrible ophadragons—had posed a serious threat. Still, Algy, Monk, Bobo, and the others whose cogitative abilities had reached and maintained maturity understood the wisdom of being prepared.

So Bobo stood watch. He was never lonely; aside from the fact that those of his people prone to severe depression had died out long before, he had for a companion one of man's best friends: Fender Fang, a mutant canine who stood four feet at the shoulders and looked something between an Alsatian and an overgrown pit bull terrier. Lovable, playful—everything one could ask for in a dog.

This particular evening, Bobo and Fender Fang embarked on their weekly trek to the settlement, ready for a night at the Batcave and a morning of trading and fun before returning to their mountain outpost. Bobo attacked the terrain with huge, confident strides, and Fender Fang bounded along beside him. As they came within a mile of the Batcave, the grinding sounds of Fiberglass Muskrat wafted out to greet their ears.

"That's 'The Trial of Proosival Roogee,' " Bobo said. "We better hurry or we'll miss all of the first set."

"Wron," Fender retorted. "Doo erly. Zdill Mugrat bragtiz."

"Think so?"

Bobo glanced back, noting the still visible, faint purple and red hues of the sunset. "Hmm. You know, you may be right."

Fender grinned happily, and the pair continued on in silence for a while. Bobo fumbled around in the pouch at his side and brought out a grenade. He tried to hide the action from Fender, to no avail. The dog bounded to him and sniffed at his clenched fist.

"Boom!" the dog said happily.

Bobo feigned irritation. "You ruin all my fun, don't you?"

Fender, undaunted, wagged his tail rapidly. "Gatch!"

"Sure," Bobo said with a laugh. He pulled the pin, leaned back, and heaved the grenade high up into the air.

Fender followed it gleefully, waited until the last moment, then took off at the descending grenade with one great leap. He caught it in his jaws while it was still ten feet off the ground, and his grin broadened as he swallowed it. He hit the ground, giggling as the thing exploded in his stomach. "Boom!" He licked his lips.

Bobo laughed. Fender leaped up and ran to him, again wagging his tail frantically. "Wunmore! Wunmore!"

Bobo raised an eyebrow. "You sure? Last time you ate so many booms that Algy had to pour a gallon of acid down your throat to get you unclogged. You don't digest metal very well, you know."

"Wunmore!" Fender insisted.

Bobo shrugged and took another grenade from his pouch.

He looked at Fender and tossed it playfully up and down in his hand. "You sure you're sure?"

Fender barked, too excited to talk coherently.

Bobo grasped the pin, then he paused. Discord hung in the air, not from Fiberglass Muskrat, but from the north. A droning hum, and it grew louder as he listened.

Fender, confused, forgot about the grenade and spun his head. "Wazzat?"

"I don't know," Bobo answered. Without luck, he tried to place the sound.

"Goming glozer!" Fender exclaimed.

"Yes."

They stood, listening. After a moment, the source of the sound topped a rise and paused, looking at them. It was tall—eight feet high, seven if the foot by which it cleared the ground was discounted. Its skin was metal, and several odd limbs of various construction and unknown purpose jutted from its shiny body. Neither Bobo nor Fender had ever seen its like.

Slowly, it began its approach.

"Wazzit?" Fender asked.

"I don't know," Bobo said, watching the thing curiously.

Fender bounded two steps toward it, and it paused again. He looked up at it. "Gatch?" he asked. "Wan gatch?"

It looked down at him stonily with one glass eye. Fender looked back at Bobo. "Try gatch. Maig fren!"

Bobo raised an eyebrow, then shrugged and pulled the pin of the grenade he held in his hand. He waited a moment, shouted, "Hey!" to the thing to draw its attention away from Fender, and tossed the grenade at it. It hit the metal shell and exploded.

Fender looked back at the thing, grinning expectantly. "Boom!" he exclaimed. He jumped when the thing played back, one of its limbs making sounds and spitting out little metal things like a rat-tat.

Bobo stood behind Fender, squinting his eyes and smiling, letting the bullets bounce off his chest.

Fender jumped about excitedly. "Maig fren!" he exclaimed. "Maig fren!"

When the thing's rat-tat finally stopped, Bobo, at Fender's insistence, tossed it another grenade. Again, the grenade exploded against its metal skin. This time, however, the thing did not play back.

For a moment, it stood still, watching them. Fender grew impatient and barked at it, then Fender heard a pop, saw a blur near the thing's head, and heard a funny boom. When the blur went away, he noticed that one of its long, straight arms had gone; only moments before, there'd been five— Fender had counted. Now there were only four.

Confused, the dog looked back at Bobo, then whined uncertainly when he saw his master sprawled on the ground, a long, straight thing sticking up from his head at an angle. It took Fender a moment to recognize the redness splattered around the area of his master as blood.

Slowly, the dog remembered the reason why he and Bobo lived in the hills, away from the others. He spun on the metal thing. Its glass eye still watched Bobo.

Fender growled and leaped. He hit the thing in its center, knocking it back. Fender grabbed at a protuberance and wrenched it away from the body with his jaws. The thing tried to back away, but Fender was upon it again in one leap, tearing away bits and pieces of metal, rending the body in his rage. He crunched the glass eye. He took the topmost part in his jaws and bit straight through the metal. The thing fell to the ground, and still Fender ravaged it, tearing and ripping until no single part of the machine was whole or attached to the body.

And at the end, Fender was crying, his spent rage turning into sorrow. He bounded over to Bobo and dripped tears onto his face, trying to lick out the thing that went into

Bobo's head through his left eye. He gripped it in his jaws and tried to pry it out gently, but the slightest movement drew more blood. Though Fender had seldom seen blood, he knew that, with this quantity, something was definitely wrong.

Bobo's right eye fluttered, and he looked up into the tearful face of his dog. "It, it didn't want to play," he said. "It went boom inside my head." His eyes closed again, and Fender sensed Bobo's body relax.

He put his ear to Bobo's chest. Nothing. He raised his head to the sky and howled in sorrow.

As gently as he could, Fender placed one great paw on the dead man's face, gripped the spear of metal, and pulled. It came out slowly, and he tossed it aside. Sadly, he licked his friend's forehead, then he wedged his head under Bobo's waist and moved forward, balancing him on his back. With mournful steps, he trudged on toward the Batcave.

V.

Slowly, in dazed agony, Philip peeled himself off the seat of the battle droid remote command center. A high-pitched noise still seared, echoed, cascaded through his mind, even though he'd torn away the headset during the first second of the noise.

His limbs spasming, he fell to the floor. Near him, the headset squealed painfully. Turn it off! he thought. "Medusa, turn it off!"

Abruptly, the squealing stopped. Except in his head . . . What the hell *was* that thing? Looked like a roughed-up, but essentially normal, very big dog.

And the man—he'd just stood there, smiling, bullets bouncing off his chest like some kind of superman.

So what do I need now? Philip wondered. Kryptonite? Damned dog had sounded like it could talk!

Maybe he'd just dreamed it all. Maybe he was still asleep. Maybe this was what happened to a hibernating human mind after a few thousand years of sensory deprivation. If so, he merely had to persuade the dream to go away, to give him back up to oblivion. . . .

"Medusa, what happened?"

"The destruction of the battle droid, of course. Data suggests mutilation by the canine. Remarkable feat. I'm still attempting to calculate the psi of the creature's jaws."

She'd stayed with him all along, Philip realized. So why hadn't she disconnected him before the droid's total destruction, before that sound had bit into his mind as if it had been the fangs of the dog?

Damned computer had let it happen! Artificial intelligence like this, he didn't need. "Medusa," he said painfully, "please try to think of my safety. That audio overload could have killed me!"

"I'm sorry, Mr. Philip," she said seductively. "You gave me no special instructions."

"I'm not supposed to have to," he mumbled, rising up to his knees. "Where would we be if I had died? What would you do then?"

"I would follow my instructions. I would wake your cousin, Martin."

Wonderful, Philip thought. Just fucking wonderful.

He rose, staggering back to Medusa's control console and collapsing in the padded seat. He reviewed what had happened with the battle droid and groaned.

Bulletproof skin . . . a dog that could rip through metal as if it were so much defenseless meat . . .

He'd probably been lucky with the explosive-tipped spear. Recalling the scene, Philip remembered how it had stuck into the man's eye. It should have gone all the way through his head and out the other side! The droid's spears could decimate buildings, blow gaping holes in mountainsides! If the spear hadn't hit the man's eye, it might have had no effect at all.

If something like that had found Tiffany . . .

What now?

VI.

The Batcave, an immense, flat building about twenty-five feet in height, lacked the clean-lined architectural sensibility of every building Tiffany had ever known. With walls of large, unfinished stone, it stretched haphazardly along one border of a small, equally chaotic group of houses and community shelters.

As Stigg ushered Tiffany into the Batcave's immense darkness, the music gripped her, its pulsating rhythms driving through, into her bones.

It was loud, but she loved it. As a teenager, she'd made a career of sneaking from the family's bosom, seeking out the darkest, punkest hangouts in Manhattan and dancing. Just dancing, her whirling body throwing off the shackles of high society, the stark, outlandish makeup on her face making her a ghoul among ghouls, a vampiric punkette with eyes of red fire supplied by Macy's Nouveau Wave line of cosmetic contact lenses. At the time, she'd known of nothing more thrilling, more dangerous, more daring. She'd never told anyone what she did when the world had thought her asleep. She'd not told even her closest friends; when they'd questioned her daytime fatigue, she'd pleaded insomnia.

Never dancing. If Mother Grant had caught even a hint of that, she would have been disowned. Perhaps even exterminated; Tiffany had heard stranger tales of the Grant clan. *Once in the blood,* they said, *you cannot leave the blood.* Not that she'd never toyed with trying. While majoring in Advanced Data Systems at MIT, Tiffany had often considered just dropping out, disappearing into the refuse of mainstream society. Dancing, becoming the music.

It had been a pipe dream. She'd never had the nerve. But, if she *was* going to leave the family, she was going to do it on her own terms. She wasn't going to get tossed out on her ear.

Dark, Tiffany thought. Darker than the Garage Club, Dementia, even the New Danceteria. Thinking of those places, Tiffany suddenly realized how utterly, permanently gone they were.

But how many years had passed? Was it truly safe for her to be out? She didn't feel any burning in her skin, any hint of radiation poisoning. But if Stigg—five feet high and three wide with pitted skin like a shriveled orange—wasn't the product of radiation-mutated genes, she couldn't imagine what was.

How many years had passed? The surface of the planet was scarred, barren, of rock and infertile yellow soil from one end of the horizon to the other. What did these people eat? She remembered Stigg and his gin—his *fifths* of gin. Who knew what he ate? Maybe nothing at all, not with a stomach that took in liquor the way his had. As she'd followed him through the dark passages below; his gait had been steady. A normal man wouldn't be able to walk after that much gin. Hell, that much gin would kill most normal men!

Maybe Stigg's skin photosynthesized or something. She'd learn soon enough, she supposed. She fought back a sudden fear that she'd soon learn something horrible, like Stigg was guiding his main course—her, Tiffany—to the caldron. He was almost short enough to be a Pygmy. . . .

No, she thought. *Think sensibly, Tiffany!*

In a way, she still didn't feel quite awake. Something inside her started to nag at her, telling her that she was *supposed* to be doing something, something important, significant. She'd wakened from her slumber. . . . How? Why? What should she do now? What would the family want her to do now?

At that thought, she laughed. She didn't *care* what the family wanted! She'd never cared. And besides, she knew what the family would want; they'd want her to hurry home and let Medusa figure things out.

Maybe Tiffany would do that, maybe she wouldn't. Stigg, so far, had been very kind. He'd found her, brought her to her senses, and, with her naked and afraid, he'd given her a robe and offered to take her out! Tiffany would never have expected the same courtesies, especially the naked and afraid parts, from any of the men she'd ever dated.

As her eyes adjusted to the darkness, Tiffany's thoughts turned outward. Inside the Batcave was a scene that reminded her of a cross between the bar scene in Lucas's *Star Wars* and the theater party in *Gremlins*. Stigg's friends, if anything, were stranger than he. Warped faces, most muscled more like gorillas than men, colors every shade of the rainbow . . . nothing particularly ugly. Some looked normal; one in particular arrested Tiffany in her tracks as soon her eyes fell on him.

He stood in the center of the Batcave's stage, bathed in stark white light that shone up from the stage's edge, an ebony rock of a man, well over seven feet tall. Not negroid, she noted, but he was blacker than that, black like oil, or wet black paint, like a Greek statue carved of obsidian. His curly, shoulder-length mane fell down over bare shoulders, and his bright blue eyes shone through the darkness like heaven spearing through the darkest thunderhead of a storm.

57

His cheekbones were high, European. His skin glistened with sweat; he was naked but for a tattered pair of blue jeans. Shimmering walls of noise rose and fell around him, but in his face was a kind of sad peace, transcendent longing—a face like a wounded, compassionate god. *Brando,* Tiffany thought, in *Apocalypse Now.* Why did she keep going back to film? she wondered. Old film . . . twenty-first-century vid had castrated itself with its own technology, its own special effects. With very rare exceptions, all space opera went back to Lucas, all watchable war vid to Coppola's timeless masterpiece with its Fallen Angel imagery, its Nietzschean angst and desperation. The death of God in a human face. In music, Jim Morrison—and in the man before her. If he was a man.

Tiffany felt his hypnotic magnetism inside her; at the same time, it attracted her and made her feel ill, as if she gazed at a manifestation of all mankind, beautiful but depraved, good but evil, peaceful, destructive, false, and naive. She couldn't tear her eyes away; as Stigg grabbed her hand and led her to a table near the stage, the man began to sing. Tiffany couldn't understand the words, but she couldn't ignore the voice. All the pained expression in the face was there in the voice as well. Around her, she sensed others gathering, but she couldn't move her eyes.

Then he looked at her, and his eyes dug into her soul, caressing it, clawing it, burning her.

Maybe its the gin, she thought frantically. She could feel the liquor's fire in her stomach. . . . Not his *eyes.* . . . This couldn't be happening. Not for real. . . .

At song's end, the man looked down and the music began to change. Tiffany had scarcely noticed the band, but she realized now that they were good. A tall, wraithlike woman with pale skin and black hair wielded the grinding, industrial guitar. Someone farther back in the shadows played a bass that weaved in and around the guitar like a gliding snake.

The drummer sounded as if he had a battalion at his fingertips, and the keyboards were dark and rhythmic, at times terrifying.

Tiffany forced her eyes away. Next to her Stigg sat, a broad smile pasted across his homely face. Behind him, more eyes, looking at her.

Stigg sensed her gaze and glanced over. "Fiberglass Muskrat!" she heard him shout over the music, but she had already turned away. The eyes behind Stigg had somehow been menacing. Watchers in the shadows, burrowing in, like the singer's eyes, to her soul.

It has to be the gin! she thought desperately. Or the lack of something. Centuries, perhaps millennia, without music, without even a sound, and now—this.

She looked back to the stage and he captured her again, carrying her into his world. This time she gave herself to him, followed him, seeking a haven in his power. In his eyes, there was hope; in those other eyes, only shadows. Unknown thoughts, unknown emotion.

Oh, Tiffany! she thought. How did you get here? What have you done?

Dreaming . . . that's it. Must be dreaming. This one— just a dream, like all the others. . . .

An eternity later (An hour? Tiffany wondered. Two hours? What did time mean in a dream?), the instruments, one by one, faded into silence. As the keyboards swirled away into nothingness, someone threw a switch, ushering in light, banishing the darkness to the fleeting world of nightmare memory.

Around Tiffany there were faces, murmuring voices, but it was the silence that echoed in her ears.

And the big man, dismounting the stage, gazed at her yet. In the light, he seemed more human. Slightly more human—his presence lingered about him like a cloak.

Stigg leaned over toward her, pointing at the singer. "Monk," he said.

"Monk," she repeated softly. Suddenly, something underneath her moved . . . her chair! She jumped up, screaming, looking back over her shoulder. The chair's back retracted into the black seat, even as she watched. Smiling eyes popped open in the center of the amorphous . . . thing.

"Benson!" Stigg squealed in the distance.

Tiffany felt all those eyes on her. Time was slowing; she was falling . . . back. Long way to the floor . . .

Black arms caught her in midfall. They wrapped about her, gently lifting her to her feet. "Benson," a voice said behind her. She looked back into his eyes; he was smiling.

Stigg laughed now; so did all the others. Tiffany looked back down at the thing that had been her chair. A broad smile had joined the eyes that watched her. . . . One of them winked.

Impossible, she thought. Comical. She felt laughter rising within her.

If any of these creatures were going to eat her, one had certainly had its chance!

VII.

Philip attacked the steak with ravenous fervor. At least Medusa could do something right; the New York Strip was just as he'd ordered it: lightly charred on the outside, pink and juicy on the inside.

That she'd synthesized the cow, or the part of the cow she'd needed, he didn't care. If the meat could fool his taste buds, his imagination could fill in the gaps. The steak was as good as any he'd had from the family's small ranch in

Texas. Better. It had been a long time . . . too long. He wished for the peace of mind to truly savor it.

What now?

The question rang over and over again in his mind.

Supermen . . . wonderdogs . . .

Tiffany lost.

What the fuck was he supposed to do now?

Just seal the damned tunnel and forget about her! She was never much goddamn use to the family anyway, always off in her own little world, babbling about modern music or, worse, political arts in their private conversations, going on like some Marxist prima donna, giving him the nails with which to crucify her and the cross for his own crucifixion if word ever got out that he'd heard her say those things and kept his mouth shut about it.

Leave her. Shut it all down and go back to sleep. . . .

Suddenly, from deeper in the complex, he heard the hiss of pumps.

"Medusa! What's happening?"

"I am reviving the militia," the computer replied.

"What?!"

"I am reviving the militia."

Philip dropped his knife and smacked the side of his head to make sure he was awake. "On whose orders?"

"Mother Grant's."

"What? You've revived her? She's awake?"

"No," Medusa replied. "I elevated her consciousness and established rapport. I told her of your sister's disappearance, your use of the battle droid, and what transpired. She instructed me to revive the militia. You are to send them out to assess the dangers to the family and liquidate any hostile denizens of the local region."

"The dog?"

"And whatever else."

Philip tried to stem the tide of his anger. "Medusa, why couldn't you just leave this to me? Why did you have to talk to her?"

"I completed my analysis of the battle droid's destruction. The event, and its tangential ramifications, cannot be ignored. In situations of extreme danger, I am instructed to establish rapport with Mother Grant. That is what I did."

Fuck! Philip thought. Authority suddenly whisked out from under his feet. . . . Next he'd have the whole goddamn family looking over his shoulder, suggesting this, criticizing that, ordering this, ordering that. . . .

Just as it had always been.

From the complex's interior, the hissing grew louder. Philip sighed and kicked back his chair. As he rose, he grabbed the rest of his steak, tore off a chunk with his teeth, threw it back on his plate, and started for the military wing to greet the wakening army.

VIII.

As Tiffany sat with Stigg and Monk, this time on a real chair, she began to grow uncomfortable again; dream or not, it kept sweeping her up, making her forget its unreality. She remained the center of attention. With Stigg rattling off their names—Nightshade, Bamph, Panda, Schlitz—they kept coming up to her, touching her hesitantly, saying things to her in some clicking, tortured mutation of a language that must once have been English. Not that that bit of intuition helped her any, but it bothered her that so many of the words made sense; the structure and grammar of the language had devolved into something resembling the made-up words of a baby learning to emulate the speech of adults.

Or maybe she had it backward. Maybe she was the infant —able to understand some words, perceptive of body language, but totally unable to put it all together into anything truly meaningful.

And not all of them looked at her kindly. Some just stared; one, Fiberglass Muskrat's guitarist, Karmen, almost glared at her. The woman stood behind Monk like a pale, white pillar of jealousy.

That was the stare that really made Tiffany nervous. She hadn't asked for Monk's attention. After a few anguished moments, one of the other musicians walked up to Karmen and put his arm around her. She turned and smiled at the newcomer, then she kissed him.

Tiffany sighed relief. So—she hadn't started a lovers' quarrel; she hadn't made that kind of enemy. Either Karmen had animosity permanently carved into her expression—not so unlikely, considering the way she played guitar—or she was angered simply because the show had stopped, because Tiffany had changed the focus of attention and interrupted her work.

It had nothing to do with anything sexual, thank God. That was the last thing she needed. Monk was interesting, but—Jesus! Where were her thoughts taking her?

She looked at Monk, held a mock microphone to her lips, and mouthed a few silent lines from *Let It Be*. Get him back onstage, she thought desperately. The singer watched her and smiled, but he shook his head.

The audience still filed up, one by one, to touch her. The line was nearly exhausted. She hoped the tension would ease then. As she motioned again to Monk, she suddenly heard a voice that made sense:

"You are from the old race," it said, "aren't you?"

Her mouth dropped open, and she turned in search of the voice. Standing next to her, a short, aged man with white hair and a kind, doglike face looked knowingly into her eyes. "Aren't you?" he repeated.

Dumbly, she nodded.

"Don't be afraid," he said. "We won't hurt you. I am called Algy. I want to be your friend, and there are many things I would like to ask you. We have lost so much of the past."

Uncertainly, she returned his smile, but as she searched for something to say, shouts rose up around the Batcave's entrance. Algy's eyes turned away from her. So did Monk's.

Then—for a moment—chaos. A mournful howl filled the cavernous building, and everyone, everything was moving as the crowd relocated itself. Tiffany moved with them, almost instinctively, immersing herself in the crowd, relieved that its attention had finally left her.

When all came to rest, they'd gathered around a huge dog who made sounds Tiffany could swear were meaningful to the others. At the dog's feet, a man lay prostate, a dark red wound where one of his eyes should have been. Monk broke from the crowd and knelt down next to the man, touching his hand to the man's neck. After a moment, he looked up at Algy. Tiffany realized the old one was still next to her.

Monk shook his head at Algy, then looked at the dog, who still made those strange, almost coherent noises. Monk was nodding, understanding the beast.

Tiffany thought of the dog and remembered the chair she'd sat on for all of Fiberglass Muskrat's first set. Evolution had definitely taken some weird turns.

Again, suddenly, the crowd was moving, out the door. Tiffany looked desperately at Algy. "What happened?" she asked.

The man cocked a bushy eyebrow and frowned. "Something terrible," he said, following the others out the door.

Tiffany raced after them. After a few steps, the rocks bit sharply into her feet and she squealed, falling to the ground. The others continued on, following the strange dog.

For some reason, one that she couldn't have explained herself, she began to cry; then, as suddenly as she'd fallen, Monk's sure hands found her, lifted her, and tossed her onto his back. She clung to him as he raced after the pack.

Overhead, a full moon lit the barren land. Tiffany could feel Monk's muscles churning rhythmically, easily, under his skin.

What had she gotten herself into?

IX.

Monk dropped her to stoop down and examine the chunks of metal strewn over the dusty ground like so much garbage. She could feel the ground shaking as Stigg and the others caught up and gathered around.

No one paid any attention to her anymore. That was good. *She should have known!*

Monk and Algy shuffled through the debris, glancing questioningly at each other. If Tiffany could find her voice, she could tell them what they wanted to know.

She should have known! From the family, there was no escape. . . .

Someone was looking for her. They wouldn't stop now. One life had already been lost, and it was her fault! And that one life wouldn't be the last.

She felt dust caking on her face and realized that she must have been crying. When she looked up from the ground, she saw legs now, with eerie faces overhead, like escapees from some genetically engineered menagerie. Except—she was the alien now. She felt it. She knew what had happened, and she knew who she was. And *how* she was: out of place, hopelessly, just as she'd been on those dance floors ten years—centuries—before.

Touch, but don't break. Like a glimpse of paradise through a dollar telescope that, after a few precious moments, slaps its metal shutter over the lens. She'd been free, damnit!

What was she thinking now? That everything had been great ten minutes before? No—but at least they hadn't hurt her, at least they'd been kind. Now God only knew what would happen next.

"Machine," Monk mumbled absently as he picked up one hunk of metal, then another. "Who made this machine?"

Algy dropped the piece he had in his hand, looked up at the clouds overhead, and sighed. "It was shaped like a man," he said wearily. "The ancients called them robots, sometimes droids or drones."

"Robots," Monk said. "Robots that kill. Why?"

"Why grenades or machine guns, Monk? They killed, too."

"Not us."

"No, but they weren't meant to kill us. They killed easily enough, though. You've seen the old picture stories."

"Yes." Monk stood, his gaze troubled, scanning the horizon over the heads of the others, who curiously picked through the remains of the machine he and Algy had cast aside.

"Monk," Algy said, standing with him. "That thing that killed Bobo went into his eye. That is a very weak place, the eye."

Monk nodded. He looked through the others and saw Tiffany. She was on her knees, motionless, her head in her hands. "She knows," Monk said softly. "Do you think she brought this machine here?"

Algy watched Tiffany a moment before answering. "No. She is afraid and sad. If she had done this, she would have run from us."

Monk frowned. "She can't run; her feet are too smooth. I had to carry her here."

Algy chuckled. "You know what I mean, my friend. Do not fear; I will talk to her. We will learn what she knows."

Through Tiffany's tears, the moonlit landscape gained a molten surrealism, the figures blurred, wavy shadows. She counted them, quickly reaching fifty before losing track of where her eyes had already traveled. Fifty moon-drenched shadows. One dead man back at the Batcave, and one supertech gunbot, battle droid, or whatever it was called, trashed beyond salvage. Had that dog done this?

So far, the score was even. If only she could feel it would stay that way . . . What now?

Monk knew she understood the causes and implications of this carnage—it was there in his shadow, the way it faced her, almost motionless, while the other shadows scurried around its feet. He knew she knew, but did he know himself? Had he seen the likes of this before, and did he know what it meant?

Did he know what war meant?

What death meant?

X.

With a flick of his tongue, Commander Eugene "Genie" Watts initiated comm with Medusa and Philip. "Found them," he said softly. He yawned at the same time; he still felt half asleep.

Philip's terse reply came immediately: "Transmit visual image!"

Genie flipped another switch with his tongue. Time passed. "Where's my sister?" Philip asked finally.

Genie squinted and shook his head. Another voice, that of Adrian Ghosting, Genie's lieutenant, joined the conversation. "There, Commander," Adrian said. "In the rear."

"Initiate opti-link."

"Acknowledged."

Slowly, Genie's visual field expanded and shifted right. Adrian guided the focal point through the gaps in the strange gathering below, then zoomed in on a lone, kneeling figure beyond. "That's her," Philip said into Adrian's ear. "Get her while you still have surprise on your side."

"No surprise, Mr. Philip," Genie said, backing out of the opti-link and panning over the ranks of the enemy. "Several have noticed us. They know we're here; they're simply waiting."

"For what?"

"You tell me."

"They don't seem to be armed. . . ." Philip's voice was weak, as if he talked to himself, letting the sentence trail off into charged silence. Empty silence—too long; Genie started to realize what must have happened. Once, this had been a sprawling, green, private, Duchess County estate. The way he'd understood it, it was supposed to be sprawling and green again before they woke from the cold sleep. Now—sprawling, yes. But bleak, everything meaningful gone in one big nuclear puff. Every woman he'd ever loved long dead, never buried, fried to cinders and, riding the crest of a wave of fire, whisked out to sea with the ashes of thirty million others? Sarah, Crystal, and Margaret— they'd all lived in the city.

How far had the war spread? The entire planet? Surely so—if not, those below would not look so weird, so warped by the fires. What had man done to mankind?

And what the hell was happening now?

"Kill them."

"What?"

Philip's voice: "Kill them! Rescue my sister, then waste those monsters!"

Just like Africa all over again, Genie thought. He'd had enough of it; that's why he'd hired on with the Grants in the first place, to get away from the bloodshed. After this one, Philip could stuff it if he planned to use Genie to wipe out the poor bastards still wandering around this godforsaken place. Maybe he'd quit anyway, no matter what. Obviously, they'd lied to him somewhere along the line.

He let himself move, mechanically now, starting forward, his laser rifle blazing. When the beams bounced harmlessly off his targets and shot into the sky, he poured on the power and kept advancing, adjusting his aim. He hit one of them—a tall, androgynous figure—full force in the face. The figure fell but still moved.

Well, he reasoned, still closing the distance, maybe he wasn't going to wipe out the poor bastards after all. He almost smiled; in a way, he'd deserved something like this for a long time.

Monk bared his chest against the barrage of red light and growled. The others around him froze and watched the silver creatures descend the slope. No one spoke until Karmen whined and fell to the dirt; Algy rushed to her side. "Her eyes, Monk! Everybody, cover your eyes!"

Monk glanced at Algy and Karmen, then jumped forward to meet the silver creatures. He grabbed one and whipped it around through the air, smashing it into two others. The three of them fell to the ground and went still.

Fender Fang leaped to Monk's side, and the others followed behind him. Snarling, Fender dove at one of the silver creatures and bit down hard, tasting hot blood for the first time since he could remember.

Stigg grinned as he watched the others play. He wanted to join them, but Tiffany looked all white and was making sad and pain sounds as if she were going to die again. He couldn't let himself get lost in the fun—she was his fault, and Stigg took care of first things first. She could die easily, he knew. It was a bad night for dying. Stigg had thought Bobo could never die.

He moved close to Tiffany, putting a hand on her shoulder. "Don't die," he said. She didn't seem to hear him.

Suddenly, a silver arm reached out of the sky and grabbed at Tiffany. Stigg grabbed the arm and squeezed, then spun it like he'd watched Monk do. The body at the end of the arm crashed into something else, then another arm came down for Tiffany.

Around him, the world became red as the silver people shone their funny magic lanterns on him. The light tickled. Loud booms started cracking the night. Stigg laughed and kept throwing the arms away. After a while, there were no more arms.

He looked, then, back at Monk. There were silver people everywhere, though half were on the ground. Some of his friends were on the ground, too, and Stigg began to grow frightened. He wasn't sure he liked this game. As he thought that, he realized that Tiffany had grown limp in his grip. He peered into her face—she was worse than when he'd first found her, and if she died it would be his fault.

She needed firewater; that had helped her before. Jumping to his feet, desperately glancing back at Monk and the others, Stigg threw Tiffany over his back and raced for his home.

Monk fought furiously, and when the few silver creatures left standing began to run, he and the others chased them down, smashed them to the ground, and brought them back to the place where Bobo had died and Fender had rended the robot. Algy tore away the silver skin from one of the creatures; there was a man inside.

"Meant to kill us," Monk said softly. Algy looked up at him and nodded.

Monk scanned the horizon for more danger before squatting down next to Algy. "Where's Tiffany?"

"Stigg has her," Algy said, his fingers probing the soft body inside the silver suit.

Monk grunted and stood. After a moment, he waved his hand over the disarrayed ranks of fallen silver warriors. "Take these back to the Batcave and keep them there. Some yet live, no?"

"Yes, some live."

Monk turned to the others. "Fender!" he commanded. "Nightshade, Grok, Weezil, and Panda—come with me! We must learn where these silver creatures lived!"

Abruptly, though he expected at the time the journey would take at least several days, Monk started up the slope.

XI.

Philip covered his ears as the painful clanging grew louder.

"Medusa! Stop them!"

"With what?"

Philip screamed and raced through the corridors, stopping short of the main blast door. The damned thing was two feet thick, and someone—something—on the outside was punching it down with his fists!

That answered one of his questions, anyway: They hadn't blasted through to Tiffany's chamber on purpose. In fact, whatever was outside had chosen the most difficult method of entrance Philip could imagine. Not that it was posing any serious problem.

Desperately, Philip turned back for the armory. On the way, the familiar hiss of pumps joined the echoing din.

"Medusa! What now, forchristsake!"

"Emergency revival procedures in process. Danger is imminent; all sleepers must waken." Her tone was bland, automatic, as if she'd regressed to lower levels of her programming.

"Shit!"

Philip reached the armory and cast about for anything that might stand a chance of helping him. Lasers were useless. Machine guns? He laughed, grabbing a shoulder-fired antitank rocket from its rack, and ran back to the blast door.

The monsters were almost in; the alloy braces that were supposed to withstand a nuclear blast were cracked and warped. Ten tons of metal were about to succumb to something that Philip had seen, something that looked like it was supposed to be human.

Hardly.

The blast door came down with a deafening crash, and the black giant, a shadow with blue lanterns for eyes, stood in the empty space. Philip leveled the rocket and fired. The impact rang like thunder through the corridors. When the smoke cleared, the giant still stood.

Dumbly, Philip dropped the rocket launcher. Behind him, he heard another voice curse softly. A human voice, one he knew: the voice of Robert, his brother.

Philip didn't even turn to look at him. He couldn't move; he could only stare, defiantly, at the approaching shadow. It had begun to move.

He stared, refusing to back down. It reached out for him, then lifted him high into the air. The world spun, then Philip felt his body smash into the side of the corridor and his world went black.

Chapter

·4·

■ DANIEL REACHED OUT and touched the moisture on the hull. It beaded around his fingers, then ran down the glass like rain on a windowpane. On the shiny parts of the hull where the water went down, he could see his reflection. As he gazed at himself, he thought of one of the short vids he'd watched the day before. One of the weird ones, a black-and-white, dreamlike thing—something Tiffany called *avant garde*. Something in the afternoon . . . it was about a woman—dreaming? He didn't know. But there was a scene in it of her, gazing from her window. He couldn't remember now whether her window had been wet or not.

Daniel's was. His sphere had lost something in its atmosphere regulation system. Nothing to worry about, the sphere had told him. It had located the problem and, it said, already repaired the faulty valve. The existing moisture would disappear in time.

Or Daniel could wipe it away and feed it back into the sphere's black box, speeding up the process.

He didn't feel like doing that right now. It was a strange feeling, being closed in by water. It made him feel like it was a pleasant, rainy day outside.

Rain in a vacuum—how he yearned to know *real* rain! To hear the crash of thunder in the air, to see lightning crackle overhead . . . The closest he'd gotten to that was the static he occasionally found in his clothes.

With the moisture on the glass, he was almost contained, in a room, or in the cabin of a ship on rough seas. Better than infinity. Right now, anything was better than that. There had been times when he'd stared out for so long that it had terrified him. The near-infinite curve of space . . . the ridiculous thing someone had once said about how someone, gazing out, unblinking, would eventually see the back of his head. All Daniel could see was infinity: black, total, immense, infinite. Terrifying, like a man seeking God and finding nothing, just empty space.

He never should have read Sartre. Or, worse, the five pages of Heidegger's *Being and Time* he'd struggled through. The being-thrusting-out-over-in-under its world or whatever. Daniel's world was the smallest he could possibly imagine. Unless Heidegger meant also where his world had been, the space through which the sphere had traveled. In that case, Daniel's world consisted of a large volume of nothing. Mark's world had been more substantial; at least the asteroid had given it an increase in mass.

Daniel shivered and shrugged off that thought. Mark was dead, so was Marsha. Perhaps it wasn't so bad. Perhaps there was a God, or something else. Perhaps his cousins had grown into something else. Become something else, something free.

Daniel didn't want to be an existentialist. In all the books, the existentialists were cold, with dead hearts that could no longer love. Most sadly, they needed other people, but, in almost every case, they had forgotten this. Daniel didn't want to forget. He, more than any existentialist ever, needed other people. Without that thought, that hope for his future, there was no point to any of it.

The day before, Daniel's sphere had informed him that he was thirteen in Earth years. In just over three years, he would walk on Earth. He hoped. What if his sphere lost something more important than an atmosphere control system valve? What then?

On Earth, they had parties and gave presents on birthdays. They were happy times. Daniel had come to dread them. When he got special birthday pictures and poems and letters from the others, it only made things worse because he just wanted to *be* with them—be able to see them up close, touch their faces, hold their hands, kiss them, hug them. . . . My God, he thought, I can't even remember what a hug feels like anymore. Tiffany had hugged him when he was very little—he could remember that, but he couldn't *feel* it anymore.

Birthdays. Soon David and Diane would have their birthdays. He wanted to give them presents, but he wasn't sure he knew how. They didn't write regular things to him anymore; they didn't write him about the vid they were watching or the music they'd been listening to or the books they were reading, the things they studied. They wrote him questions, constantly, incessantly. What did Tiffany say about this? What happened to Philip? Did Tiffany love Philip? Why would Mother Grant want Philip's balls for breakfast? Were Rachel and Jan there, too? Asleep?

Why would a dog want a grenade to explode in his stomach?

Who was Henna? Stigg's girlfriend?

Did Tiffany become Monk's girlfriend? Stigg's girlfriend?

What happened to Genie? Did he die?

Did Karmen die?

What happened next?

Why are we here?

Why did you stop writing?!

He hadn't written any more of Tiffany's story in a year and a half. Well—he'd tried. So many times he couldn't count. But it was so complicated. He'd tried to do too much with what he already had; he'd gotten into too many people's minds and, in doing so, lost track of his own.

He could tell them everything they really needed to know in a few pages, but that wouldn't be right. Tiffany wanted them to understand, and he still wasn't sure he did. Or maybe he did and that was part of the problem. Maybe he just couldn't understand that people could do some of things they obviously did. Maybe he couldn't understand things like greed, jealousy, pride, and envy. Nevertheless, he was learning, but sometimes, when he realized this, he almost wished he was three again, playing games with the sphere, watching cartoons, and learning how to read.

Back then, Tiffany had come to him every night in his dreams. Now he dreamed mostly about stars and empty space. And Stigg; he dreamed about Stigg a lot. Stigg lived in darkness, just like Daniel.

It wasn't as though he hadn't written, hadn't answered their questions. He'd done that almost constantly; this was one reason why he hadn't been able to write any more. Some of the letters, especially Monica's, had taken him days to answer. Somewhere along the line, Daniel had told them that Tiffany had given him pictures along with her words, and Monica wanted him to describe every one in minute detail. He'd do that, send it to her, she'd draw it, send it back, and he'd tell her how close she was, send it back, and she'd draw it again. . . .

Two Earth months before, Daniel had found out that his sphere could copy onto paper. Whenever Daniel thought about anger, he now thought about how he'd felt right after the sphere had told him that. He'd felt like screaming, pounding through the sphere's hull, grabbing it, and heaving it violently off-course, into the sun. The goddamned thing could *copy!* He'd actually cursed at it, worse, probably, than all the cursing Tiffany did in her story.

The sphere could *copy!* He still got mad if he thought about it long enough. Of course, the sphere had an excuse: its programming. Jan and Tiffany had decided that if their children were pampered during their education, they'd never really learn how to write or draw, and that was important. Daniel supposed that was true, and, once he'd realized that his mother had made the decision, he could get only so mad; he just wished he'd learned about it sooner. He hadn't *minded* describing the pictures for Monica, but it had never been very easy.

The writing, though—that would have been easier, too. The first thing he'd done was get copies of the pictures for Monica; then he'd gotten the first part of Tiffany's story back from David, who had just read it for the ninth time. Daniel read it to his sphere, then had the sphere copy it to paper four times so they would all have a fresh, clean printout.

For a while, after that, things had gotten worse. Now he could have the sphere copy Tiffany's own words for everybody, and that would be the end of it. Thankfully (or was he really glad things had worked out this way?), Monica had persuaded the others to wait. She'd told them that her brother had invested four years of his life trying to puzzle this story out for them while they had gone on with their learning and poetry and whatever else they'd wanted to do. Daniel had had a responsibility, and he'd made it his life. It had become his life. They shouldn't want so quickly to take it away from him. After all, they still had three more years before Earth. It wasn't as if they hadn't time to be patient.

And wasn't the mystery itself worth something? Wasn't it, at times, the only thing that made their lives worth living?

Monica had won. Daniel had agreed that, after he'd finished, they could have Tiffany's own words if they still wanted them. Or most of them, except the ones that were for him alone.

So why was he still not writing? He'd read and reread his copy of the already written part. He felt pretty good about it; it wasn't so bad, though, while it was away from him, he'd begun to fear that it was terrible. He'd been saved, he realized, by Tiffany because so much of what he'd written had been a rearranging of Tiffany's words, her talk about her feelings, her talk about others and their feelings and personalities. Sure, Daniel had filled in some big blanks writing about some of the conversations, like the one among Algy, Monk, and Stigg, and ones Philip had with Medusa, but all that fit the characters involved as Tiffany had described them. Daniel's biggest liberty, as he saw it, was Philip's thinking about abandoning Tiffany. Daniel could never know something like that for sure, but it still made a lot of sense when he thought about Philip.

And the long arguments with the sphere on language had helped him as well. He supposed that he hadn't done so badly for an eleven-year-old.

Still, lately, he'd read a *lot,* and he'd found it hard not to feel like a very bad writer after reading things by people like Asherman and Quint, Hemingway, and Capote . . . especially Capote. He never felt he could grasp everything that Capote had written; when he tried to study the way the man had done it, the poetry in the way he'd put one word after another, he could seldom do more than read and cry.

He'd also listened to lots of music and watched lots of vid. Tiffany had given him a long list of vid she wanted him to study because she felt that that was the best way he could really see Earth, what it had been, its history, and why it had become what it had become. Through vid, she said, he could see both the beauty and the horror at the heart of every man's soul. Through one good piece of art, she said, one could learn more than from all the dry histories of mankind compiled by scholars. At first, Daniel hadn't been able to understand his mother's fascination, her adulation, of old work from the twentieth century. Daniel had a soft spot in his heart for the high-tech animated fantasies that had proliferated in the late 2060s, beautiful, immense productions that could never had been made the previous century. But only one of those—*Melnibone Surfacing*—had made Tiffany's list. As for other twenty-first-century vid, she'd talked about *The Lost History of Kate McCloud*, Mercy Night-Wilmington's last vid, and *Emergence*. Not much else. *Emergence* was one of Daniel's favorites because its heroine was a lot like him and Monica and Diane and David: young, like them, very intelligent, and very alone.

Over the past few days, Daniel had watched two vids from Tiffany's list over and over again. The first, *Mishima*, was a beautiful, sad thing about a writer who had killed himself for reasons that Daniel could scarcely begin to understand. He wished terribly that he could talk to Tiffany about it.

The second vid, *Merry Christmas, Mr. Lawrence*, puzzled him in a similar way, though he'd found that watching this one made *Mishima* a little easier to understand. Like *Mishima, Merry Christmas, Mr. Lawrence* was about the Japanese—Oriental earthlings very different from Tiffany and her people. That, he thought, was what attracted him to them. In a way, they were as different as Monk and Stigg and the others. And *Merry Christmas, Mr. Lawrence* helped him understand the part of Tiffany's story that he had to write next. The vid examined a clashing of cultures, with one culture holding the other captive. But the prisoners, in their minds, refused to surrender, and most refused even to change.

And so Daniel began his work anew. He wrote and re-wrote and time passed. For David's and Diane's birthdays, he made them copies of all of David's poems that he'd had his sphere memorize over the years. Monica told him that doing that made Diane happier than anything could, short of David's salvation.

They still had no way to fix David's sphere's vector correction system.

Slowly, the next part of Tiffany's story began to take shape under Daniel's pen. . . .

·EARTH·

PART TWO

I.

Dreaming.

Yes . . . like, on a hot afternoon, an Acapulco beach, skin, drenched with coconut oil, baking a delicious brown.

Release the catch and dream.

Deeper.

Clouds like cotton rock over the ocean. Mountains of down cliffs. Do the gulls rest there? Can't land on the sea . . . too soft, water.

Deeper. The sun glides, and the white mountains grow gold and deepen, roots like feathery fishtails sinking into the sea. Distant engines roar—shut them out! The stage on the horizon—too distant to hear; the life in the sky more fleeting and tragic than the human day (yet the sky's dance over water had played countless billion times since the planet's first rains, each show unique and different from the last; one day mountains, the next heavenly trees or a host of mushroom tops descending in file into the sunset). Had the clouds ever held the same shapes twice?

No. *History never repeats*. Patterns, yes, but the forms were humanity's invention. The universe had the annoying habit of breaking human rules.

Too rational—she must be waking. . . .

Eyes. Light? No—darkness. Underground, on her back. Where was she?

The long sleep, Tiffany. Don't forget it. . . .

That last nightmare, with the orange rock man, the talking dog, and the black Adonis . . . the worst yet! When would this end? How many centuries to go? How many more dreams?

Sleep again. Don't wait for Medusa to increase the . . . the whatever it was. The *soma*, the nectar of sleep, of escape.

To escape this dream of dreaming . . .

Reach back, past the beginning, past the first new dream, past all the old. And all the rest. Past Medusa and Mother Grant's exodus and those horrible, sad, aching days of good-byes when she'd prayed for, but never found, the will to run to some distant haven, a Japanese temple or some Tibetan cave where the money couldn't chase her.

Where she couldn't touch the money. None of it, not a dollar . . . Better to be shrinkwrapped and thawed out in the Golden Age of some future civilization?

No, past that. Past the cocoon and her years under the AI Development System at MIT as a counteranalyst (What a laugh! As if it were possible for subgenius humans to do anything useful in data processing anymore.) Past the university, school, and a childhood of myopic fantasies of dollhouses and Gypsies on horseback. The unicorn days when chivalry was real . . .

. . . that was the future! The gallant prince with his golden sword that would free her from the evil minions of the Dragon Queen.

No—too corny. Past that, too. Past holographic dinner dates at Tabatha's on Broadway ("Don't touch! Don't break the magic!"), past giggles in a floating playpen, past her birth, flyers, lasers, spaceships, and computers.

To Acapulco, the beach to herself, the fires of the sun digging deep into her skin. The days of real coconut oil, before the coconut trees went extinct.

Oh! Were it only true!

Why hadn't Medusa knocked her back out yet?

Never mind—build a new dream. She still had sleep— her body felt so distant—and it would fade farther, sleep deepening in the end.

It always did.

II.

The memory twisted in, out of the dark silence, but a *real* memory, like a dream because he hadn't fully wakened; the waking world of his memory merged with the abstract colors of dream to give him this twilit reality. The sun glistening on the pool—he was *there*. He could *see* her, see her smiling, golden brown eyes, hear her laugh, feel her skin, smell the jasmine and honeysuckle in her hair, her blond cascade that flirted with the breeze and tickled his arm as he touched his fingers to her lips.

Her name was Crystal, like an enchantment or something, a fairy-tale princess, only he knew her life had fallen somewhat short of fantasy perfection. She'd been a streetwise whore when he'd met her. Hurt, but not jaded—that in itself had amazed him. The laughter in her eyes was real.

So was her touch. He was there, goddamnit! *Don't let this half dream end.* . . .

He kissed her, and she caressed his cheek.

He would leave her the next day. God, the thoughts he'd had! He loved her like he'd never loved before, pouring out his heart as if each breath were his last.

He touched her breast, and she sighed, easing back onto the grass.

Perfect love, he thought as he kissed her again. She would never lose this, never feel it whisked away on the doubts, fears, and jealousies of human relationships, never have it sundered by a suspicion of infidelity, a stray strand of hair, a lingering trace of unfamiliar perfume. Enshrined, it was inviolate, eternal, perfect—the stuff of romance.

The power he felt with each touch! She would never forget this tenderness, this sweet, longing passion. She would ache for it again and again, but in that aching she would know she was worthy of such a perfect love. For a girl who had once been a prostitute, that was the greatest gift a man could provide.

As he joined with her, as they came together, he could see his life like a book read back to front, eyes lingering over the destiny-blind drama of his last day. This was his farewell note. . . .

He began to wake—*he'd been a fool.* . . . But he summoned the dream back, and he loved her more passionately, more completely, until he strained and strained and the dream faded and fled. . . .

He really had left her.

That was yesterday, Genie realized, waking fully. Yesterday, all that had really happened. Yesterday—thousands, millions of other yesterdays had passed while he'd slept.

He sat, his back rubbing up against the rough-hewn stone, rock against rock. How many thousands of years? he wondered.

He'd left them all behind, in any case. Crystal—long since dead. She must have heard of his death, the rigged one, the flyer accident over the Atlantic or whatever else the Grants had cooked up.

No turning back now. . . .

The Grant exodus had been quite secret. He understood the logic: Why give all mankind a technology that was good only for escaping from itself? Putting a world full of problems asleep for a few thousand years wouldn't make the problems go away. He knew that to be true; the oldest, hardest parts of him knew it beyond all doubt. Mankind had reached and passed some kind of political saturation point in the middle of the twentieth century, and, since then, the world had been trapped in national, social, and religious structures not fit for the nuclear age. And yet the structures had refused to change, balancing the fate of each day on the precipice of nuclear hell, with spiraling technology only continuing to worsen the situation. Independent entities, corporations, churches, charismatic radicals, terrorist groups—anyone capable of amassing funds—could collect power enough to demolish a city or even a small country, things the greatest armies of two centuries before could never have dreamed of accomplishing. The last Genie had heard, the United Nations had all but given up its attempts to police the nuclear black market; they'd even admitted their list of Third World and independent nuclear powers to be several years out of date. And yet Genie had understood the tragedy in that. He'd heard and seen enough to know that what international peace organizations couldn't know, the old superpowers did. You'd never hear about all of it on the news: Just, one day, there'd be group of Muslims in Cairo or a splinter of one of the African independence groups mouthing off about how they could wipe out Washington or Moscow or Tokyo; then, the day after, silence. Or another State Department Fallout Advisory for international travelers. And, for the time, Washington, Moscow, and Tokyo would go on.

They used their satellites, of course. Amazing they had any left after all the secret space wars that sometimes lit up the night sky like unannounced meteor showers. Lose one, send another up . . . as long as the tax money kept pouring in, there wasn't a problem. But the system couldn't be broken apart—no, for how could a country survive without spying on its people and the rest of the world? Without being able to discover and annihilate a mobile missile on its launch pad? Without being able to annihilate the satellite waiting to annihilate the satellite waiting to annihilate mobile missiles on their launch pads?

A fallible system, surely, the San Francisco Holocaust of 2071 being the most recent proof, but no one had yet come up with an answer that worked. And so the human race had become a dragon, its flames so out of control that it could only burn itself.

And he—Genie—had grown up with but one dream: to be a mercenary. Within himself, he supposed, lurked all the problems of mankind in microcosm. Only as a warrior could he envision himself free, a man. As a teenager, he'd tried to picture himself as an architect, an engineer, even as a hardened, bruised veteran of that most hallowed form of tame warfare, American football. Each time, as he'd dress himself up in his mind, his face would melt and he'd become featureless, just another insignificant scrap of futile existence. Only by staking his life on his decisions, on forces within himself, could he make his image of himself feel real.

Even then he'd known the workings of the world to be

madness. He'd thought, perhaps by accepting the madness, becoming a functional part of it, that it might one day reveal itself to him as something more, a slave to some higher, eternal principle. If not, then it followed that the madness itself was the higher principle, the closest mankind would ever get to God. Or reality, at least.

So he'd taught himself to fight. Not hard, that, considering how difficult it would have been to survive grade-school recess without understanding the value of an aggressive fist. Kids had to fight, and they knew it; only adults pretended it wasn't necessary. The children were certainly wiser. Closer to the reality, too young to know how to shield themselves from the madness with lies named peace, money, pity, and tolerance. Genie had never met a man with tolerance in the truest sense of the word. Never heard of one, in fact—even Christ didn't qualify. The best a man could hope for was compassion. For what good that did. Hard to love someone when they'd just as soon blow up your hometown as set foot on its streets.

No, Genie had sought the madness, and the madness had embraced him. He'd fought, killed, and nearly been killed so many times that he'd lost count. He'd fought the Chinese in India and the Indos in Australia during the late 2060s. He'd spent the early 2070s commanding guerrillas for the United Nations of Africa. That, he guessed, was when it had begun to get to him, and the contract offer to work for Grant T & E had come none too soon. Fairly laid back, until this. At least he'd found—and left behind—some love before the madness had come to a head. Love, he'd thought, the elusive yin aspect of the yang of warfare. He'd always thought it strange that the Chinese clothed the yin in darkness and the active yang in light. Never seemed that way in reality, but the reality was madness. Feminine dark, masculine light . . . love in the night, war at sunrise: Maybe the Zen Buddhists could understand it; he never could.

Funny—that thought. It wasn't true, not really. When he'd dreamed of being a mercenary, when he'd reached out to grasp the madness, he had understood. He hadn't known, at the time, the meaning of the Buddhist symbol, but he certainly would have understood it. Now he couldn't; he'd lost that grasp on reality, the old reality.

As Genie recalled all his old cynicism, he could barely suppress his laughter at himself. There he'd been, in an insane world, searching for some higher principle at the very heart of the insanity. He'd definitely mellowed. Forget the Buddhism and the reasoning; the world he'd known was gone now, obliterated. With it, hopefully, the madness. . . . True, he'd lost Crystal, but he'd done the best he could, and he'd had to escape. No other way to lay full claim to his own sanity. But had he succeeded? What about the previous night? Invincible mutations of what must once have been human? Lasers designed to pierce reflective armor bouncing off living skin? Where was he now? Occasionally, out in the darkness around him, something moved.

Movement . . . Genie sat still. No point in trying to go anywhere if he couldn't see where the hell he was. It was too damned dark to do anything but think. He wasn't even sure if he was in a cave, or a building. Whoever put him there would surely throw on a light in the end, unless they could see in this inky shit.

Jesus, what had happened? After the bombs snuffed out the last recognizable outpost of civilization? How long had the world gone on after he'd left it? A week? A month? A few years? Had Luck tossed its hat into the ring enough times for Crystal to live out her life to some sort of natural end, or had it gone, truly, as he'd envisioned the night before, the nuclear winds sweeping her with all his old lovers out over the Atlantic in one massive cloud of radiation and death?

He rubbed his back roughly against the rock. Raw rock, like a cave. But the air felt too dry, and too warm. Caves were never warm, and all he wore was the thin, synth-cotton body liner of his battlesuit. Would freeze to death in a cave. . . .

Distinct sounds now—out in the darkness, to his left. Someone wimpered, and moved, crawling over the rock. The sounds of the man, if indeed it was a man, echoed faintly in the distance. The crawler moved away, then crashed into something and screamed. Metal chinked against metal—old-fashioned barbed wire, Genie knew its sound, and its bite, well.

So they were definitely prisoners; he knew that for certain now. How many of his men were with him?

He started to push himself forward, then fell back against the rock. What difference did it make what he did at this moment? It wasn't as if he knew enough yet to rally the troops for a daring escape, and he didn't think it likely that many of his men would be in any shape to try anything daring for a while. And, of course, it would be worse than pointless if any of his captors were actually watching him.

He called up their images from the night before (or was this simply later, the same night?). Children—they'd seemed like wild children, at least those of them who had looked human. Like the beasty little heathens in *Lord of the Flies,* maybe a little larger. Even the big black one, the obvious leader, had seemed confused, delaying the counterattack long enough to have ensured his death, had that been something prepared to follow naturally after a laser blast that could blow a hole in the chest of a normal man. Maybe there had been something wrong with the lasers. . . . No, he remembered one reflected beam flickering hotly up the arm of one of his men, he remembered the man's gasp of pain over the comm-link just before his own world had gone black. He still didn't know what had hit him. That had never happened before, but he'd be an idiot to think that he hadn't seen what he knew he had.

Out there in the darkness . . . perhaps there lurked the answers to all his old questions, the end to the madness. Beings of rocklike flesh, like the human vision of an immortal, indestructible soul. Spirits free from fear of death, before which he was little more than a helpless Neanderthal. Once, he'd tried to envision *Homo superior* and failed, adopting the Clarke/Sturgeon Postulate of an evolutionary gestalt like everybody else. Obviously, something had gone a little awry on that one. Nobody had ever concluded what qualities would ensure the survival of the fittest in an irradiated world. Maybe he'd get to see now, firsthand. Did he really want to find out?

Yes, he did. In a way, it was all developing into some subtle, cosmic joke, as if God had taken him, whisked him from his world, and said, "Here, my boy—here are your answers. Enjoy them for a while, for you've paid dearly for your knowledge."

Cackling laughter then—God was ever the sadist.

III.

Running water.

That wasn't right; waves were supposed to crash or lap or something. Cyclical, like the moon, the incessant breath of the ocean that had washed life upon the shore and stolen it away again. Or so the sailors said, but this water ran, like a stream. And what had happened to the gulls?

Definitely something wrong. She couldn't feel the sun anymore, and the distant clouds grew brown and folded back into the sky. She lay on her back now; she was supposed to be on her belly.

What was happening to her dream? She rolled to her right and stony, icy fingers stabbed at her side; she felt the goose bumps ripple all the way down to her toes as she turned violently away.

She was sure as hell awake now! Feel her body—cold, yes—rock underneath, but kept away in places by some thin fabric, a robe because it covered her arms, one breast, and she could feel it under her calves. Her other breast stood free in the cold air, and the backs of her heels rested against the rock.

The sound of running water remained constant, began to reverberate. A gentle sea of yellow lapped at the edge of one closed eyelid. She tried to make it go away, make the dream change; the lazy beach afternoon hadn't had time to mature into a mysterious, candlelit evening. . . . She felt too damned awake, but she couldn't be: She knew this robe, even without seeing it. It was part of that horrible other dream, the one in which she'd wakened and gone out into the world alone, only to find she couldn't escape. Couldn't be real; those she'd met were impossible, the stuff of imagination, some mental trick she'd played on herself with Freudian mirrors, some nightmare she'd dredged up with which to torture herself, a nightmare peopled by the strong, pure, and innocent—negatives of her own weaknesses, her uncertainties, her impotence in the face of decision. She needed decisions now, and the right ones. If not—if she lost to this nightmare—it could keep her for centuries. She'd rather be dead.

She *would* be dead if she didn't get warm. What was that light? Fire? Why couldn't she hear anybody else nearby? Just the sound of running water . . . She forced open her eyes.

A beam of light on her left shot up like a pillar that ended in a wide, glittering circle twenty feet above her. She turned her head toward the source: a sun lantern, solar-charged, disposable, so they said, if you could burn it the ten light-years they boasted in the vidverts. Where had *that* come from? Oh, yes—she remembered: Stigg. Same nightmare now for certain, only it had a new twist: She was free and alone; she could start it over.

That wasn't such a bad thought, considering the state of things she'd left behind before dreaming her way onto that beach. Maybe she could just close her eyes again and dream herself back? No—she felt too here, and, anyway, she had the unnerving feeling that she'd only find herself jerked back into this world, most likely into circumstances much worse. At least now she had herself to herself, and no sign at all of that endless cast of warped negative selves designed to confuse her. She had the peace now to recollect and analyze. . . . What part of her was Stigg not? Not the brooding part, surely; definitely not her inability to throw back a fifth of gin and remain standing. And Monk? What was he not? Not her indecision or her lack of presence. Not her lack of talent. . . .

Forget that—too depressing, and definitely not the way to escape this nightmare; it was more like wallowing in it. Try a different approach: What did she have? Well, she had herself (still), and the sun lantern. That in itself almost made her smile; something inside her was on her side. This wasn't all self-flagellation because some part of her wanted her to win, some part of her had remembered the lantern and summoned it up to stand at her side and show her its light. At any rate, she'd be in helluva state without it.

What else did she have? The robe (could've dreamed up something warmer, though; draw it tighter, tie the sash—a little better at least) and the cave (not much use except that she had it to herself—she hoped). Yes—and the stream (good for nothing, or did she actually feel thirsty?). What else? Slowly she stood up, grabbed the sun lantern, and shone the light about her. The cave, its axis marked by the stream, was long but quite thin. Geologically, she guessed it to be recent history; it lacked the spectacular sort of mineral deposits that had once made places like Mammoth Cave and Carlsbad Caverns massive tourist attractions. Well, no, that sort of thing took more than just time, didn't it?

She shook the thought from her head and took a step forward. Along the rock walls, several dark recesses refused to reveal their natures from where she stood; she would have to go exploring soon—any or all could be passages. Did she want to go back down the one through which she'd come there? She didn't know which one. . . . But she'd dreamed herself there, hadn't she? She hadn't needed a passage for that. What if all the recesses led to dead ends? What if the stream was her only exit? She thought of the water and swallowed, growing acutely aware of her thirst at the same time. Suppressing her fears, she knelt at the stream and drank greedily with cupped hands. The water was cold and clean; she rubbed her face with wet hands, then dried both on the robe. The cloth smelled musty and old, and her ragged fingernails kept catching in the threads. Why had she dreamed herself broken nails? She wished she'd remembered a file . . . and a brush. If the quivering reflection in the water before her was any indication, she was a mess.

After exploration, she had three choices for exit, four if she wanted to count the stream. None of passageways looked much different from the next; she chose the one she did because, standing inside its entrance, the air felt a little less forbiddingly frigid. The difference was slight; she could have imagined it, but it was all she had to go on. As she started forward, her mind raced ahead, finding a boiling, furnacelike lava pit at her journey's end. She chuckled grimly at the thought; at least it would be warm.

So she walked. The passageway was quite even, almost

smooth, as if it had been carved by Nature for bare human feet. What a strange dream! Nothing at all like any of the others; she tried to pick back through the centuries of hallucinogenic memory. . . . Before they'd done what they did, the biotechs had told them they wouldn't dream except during brief periods when the cryogenic systems had to increase biological activity to verify that everything continued to function properly. What they hadn't been told was how often that might happen. As far as Tiffany knew, it seemed to go on forever. Of course, a thousand years was like a human forever, so several of those would seem more. Dreaming for a couple or three days once or twice a century would still add up to a lot of dreamtime.

This was the worst, though. This was more real, even more real than the one in which she'd gone to that posh party and mingled with the socialites, everyone draped in incredibly expensive evening dress. She'd met some man who'd claimed to be Byron—not a reincarnation, but *the* Lord Byron. He'd lounged with her against a wall, making lewd remarks about the pretentious, spoiled heiresses passing by with their slightly drunk financiers and leery-eyed gigolos. She'd enjoyed it immensely; what he'd said, she'd thought countless times over, every time she'd ever conceded to show up at those affairs. In that dream he'd been her alter ego, her disgust clothed in mystery—mystery because he'd dared to speak bravely—flippantly, actually—without apparent fear or regret. She'd never known how to do that. But why Byron? She'd hardly been a literary scholar, and she'd learned more of the nineteenth-century poet through Ken Russell's *Gothic* than from anywhere else. . . . Anyway, after endless hours talking, with the evening drawing to a close, he'd turned to her and said the world would end within the minute. He'd clutched at her, kissed her passionately. She'd felt his hand moving up the inside of her thigh, then the world had exploded.

The bomb—it haunted many of her dreams, even the ones before the deep sleep. Always she would either wake, or survive to see the horrors of the aftermath. In the Byron dream, he'd ignited in her arms, but she'd survived to wander out of the chaotic party and into the streets. Her own flesh on fire, she'd raced across the rubble, finding none alive but those emerging from their subway homes to claim the ruins of the city that had shunned them and chased them underground.

That dream had been horrible, at least in its ending. So real, as well, except for Byron as Byron and except for her survival. This one, though . . . much weirder in ways; perhaps it felt more real because it was the first in which she'd dreamed of waking up? The first that fit, roughly, her actual reality?

Tiffany's journey down the smooth passageway was, in fact, quite brief. It ended, with perfect dramatic precision, just as her last thought—the one about "actual reality"—blossomed into wholeness. It ended just after she stooped to shine the sun lantern into a mysterious hole at the bottom of one side of the corridor. She followed the light in and discovered a bare-walled room. Shortly thereafter, the sun lantern's beam found an open, empty cryogenic module.

She'd dreamed a dream of waking into a harsh new world. Now she'd dreamed herself home.

IV.

Stigg held his breath. He'd been holding it for a long time—he didn't know how long; maybe it was morning outside already. Once, he'd held his breath for a whole day, but he'd wanted to then; he'd tried to then—that was what he'd been doing, trying to hold his breath for a whole day. Now he didn't want to; he wanted to breathe. But he couldn't breathe because if he did, whoever it was who had snuck down to his home and hid there, waiting for him, would know that he was just around the corner.

Stigg knew someone was there because he could hear him moving around on Stigg's wooden bed. Aside from that, the someone had a magic candle and kept flicking it on and off and making it dance on the rock wall across from Stigg. Right now, the someone was drinking—probably Stigg's own firewater that he'd had to give Algy a whole box of boom-balls for!

He had to do something. Holding his breath wasn't any fun at all this time. And Tiffany was still back at his secret river, waiting for him. She could be dead by now! He needed his firewater to wake her up again, but if the someone was drinking his firewater, maybe all his firewater, then he wouldn't be able to do anything and Tiffany would definitely die and it would be all his fault.

Who could it be, waiting for him in his home? Surely one of his friends, but they'd come to find him and Tiffany. Somehow, he knew that for certain. He'd taken Tiffany up to see Monk and Fiberglass Muskrat, and look what had happened! Bobo *dead*? Other people dead? Silver people all over the place, and Tiffany dying again . . . he wasn't going to let that happen again. He'd wanted it to be just him and Tiffany until he could think about it all and figure out what had happened, but things kept coming so fast, he didn't have time to think. At least he'd been smart and hadn't brought Tiffany here. As far as Tiffany was concerned, Stigg was still in control.

That was it! Stigg was in control. Why was he worried that someone would take her if he didn't have her? He could pretend he didn't know where she was, then the someone would go away and Stigg could get what was left of his firewater and take it to Tiffany so she wouldn't die! Why hadn't he figured that out before?

Wearing a silly smile, Stigg jumped around the corner and into his home. "'Sprise!" he exclaimed. The someone's magic lantern flashed brightly into his eyes.

"Stigg," said Henna's voice. "Where have you been? I've been waiting forever!"

"Uh—got lost? Yes, Stigg got lost."

Henna lowered the light beam, then set it down next to her so it shone up. She looked very pretty like that in the light, Stigg realized. She had very smooth skin, almost as smooth as Tiffany's, and it was light green, like her hair. Her eyes were dark brown and soft; Stigg had always loved those eyes.

"You're not the only one, Stigg," Henna said, sighing. "Karmen can't see anything anymore, even with light. And Bamph and Weezil are dead."

"Like Bobo?"

Henna nodded.

Stigg swallowed hard. "Monk and Algy," he said slowly, "think it's Tiffany's fault, but it isn't. It's Stigg's. They shouldn't be mad at Tiffany."

"Oh, Stigg," Henna said. Her voice was very sad. "Monk didn't blame you, and he didn't blame Tiffany, either." She paused, looking at him. "Come here," she said finally.

Stigg watched her pat the space on his pallet between her legs. After a moment, he stepped forward and sat there, pressing himself back against her. Her arms wrapped around him, and she spoke softly. "Monk told me you might be afraid," she said. "Don't be, Stigg, please. He sent me for you and Tiffany. Where is she?"

Stigg tried not to think of Henna's hands; they were moving up and down his arm. He had to pretend—he had to concentrate! "She—she ran away."

"Where?"

"I don't know. She ran, and Stigg couldn't catch her. She runs very fast."

"She can't run, Stigg," Henna said, her fingers still absently stroking his arm. "Monk had to carry her to where Bobo died. Remember?"

"Stigg remembers."

"You never did know how to lie, darling. Where is she?"

"Don't know," Stigg said after a moment.

"Monk won't hurt her. He said to tell you that Tiffany is Monk's friend, too. Monk needs all his friends now, Stigg, even you. He said he needs Tiffany so she can tell him who else his friends are."

"Monk knows who his friends are! Everybody is Monk's friend!"

"No, Stigg. You left, remember? After you left, Monk found more people like Tiffany inside the silver people. And he found even more later. And the silver people tried to kill Monk; they tried to kill everybody. Monk needs Tiffany to explain it all. Algy can talk to her, and find things out."

"More people like Tiffany?"

"Lots more. After we go get Tiffany," she said, moving her hand under his arm and around his waist, "we can go see them. Where is she?" Her hand slipped lower.

Stigg gasped. "Secret river," he mumbled.

"Let's go then," Henna said, moving her hand back up to his waist.

"Where?"

"To get Tiffany!"

"Stigg doesn't know where she is! Stigg told you!"

"She's at the secret river."

"How did you know?"

Henna eased back so that Stigg's head fell between her breasts. She looked down into his eyes. "You just told me, darling. Now, come—there's no time to waste."

"Monk promised he wouldn't hurt her?"

"Yes, he promised. I promise, too."

She smiled at him, and Stigg remembered how much he loved that smile. He drank it in for a moment, then, grudgingly, he rose and helped her up.

He started out, then paused, reaching back and grabbing several bottles of firewater from the case Algy had traded him. He looked at Henna. "So she doesn't die," he said, moving out into the darkness.

V.

Someone threw on the lights shortly after sunrise. Genie had watched the dawn spear through the darkness in the form of two pale, thin beams overhead. In the light, he'd watched dust dance; at least that much about the planet had remained constant—eternal dust, ready to rise at the air's beckoning, ready to settle over life's decay.

Then the lights came on, everywhere, like beasts devouring the feeble fingers the sun had innocently inserted through minute gaps in the masonry. The poetry of dawn, in Genie's memory, had never been so fleeting. As he squeezed his eyes shut and tried to recoil, even farther, from the dazzling blue and white afterimages, he wondered if the shock of birth was so disturbing. In truth, he'd spent his last hours as if in a womb, a world of gentle darkness in which all sound had only hinted at meaning, and all meaning, fragmentary and consumed by the darkness, had remained suspended, waiting for the clarity—the completeness—that only light could provide. Now he could look around. Now he could be forced to act.

Other voices groaned as Genie forced himself to look out. His eyes met other eyes directly ahead, beyond the rolls of barbed wire, maybe thirty feet ahead: a row of eyes, all belonging to those he had seen under moonlight the night before. In the day, their spectacle appeared somewhat more tragic, less like a carnival, more like the physical maladies he'd seen inflicted on life by years of despair and suffering. Except for the eyes—the eyes were innocent. Cautious and curious, but still innocent. Patient, too, and strangely absent of hate. (They *should* hate us, he thought. We attacked without provocation, and we *must* have at least injured some of them. They should hate us. . . .) He looked at them, forcing a smile; several actually smiled back.

Glancing to his left, Genie saw what was left of his men, and—yet another surprise—that part of the Grant clan he'd been charged with defending. Reflexively, he rubbed his eyes and opened them again: Yes, there was Mr. Philip himself, trying to pull himself up on one elbow, groggily looking around. How had he ended up here? Genie had been certain the man was still tucked safely away in the cryo-complex, consulting with Medusa, trying to come up with some other, hopefully less stupid, plan of attack. But everyone was here—Philip, his brothers, his sisters, their aunt, uncle, and cousins—his eyes found them all. He was less lucky with his men; he'd started with thirty-three, and he had maybe fifteen left, and several of the survivors looked like they probably wouldn't make it through the morning. All the others—dead?

He grunted, watching Philip Tyler-Grant and wondering why on earth he'd let the overeducated, overfed, and undersexed bastard persuade him to take on that battle without doing a little scouting on his own, in his own way. The cobwebs of centuries-long sleep had clouded his mind, that was true, but he knew better than that. When Genie had joined up with Grant T & E, Philip had only just shed his mantle of collegiate immaturity. Nevertheless, Mother Grant had already handpicked him as the grandson to inherit the company. Excepting little Robert Travis, who'd then been all of six, all of her sons had already evolved into spoiled sybarites, and the old woman had confided to Genie that Philip alone of all her descendants had displayed the even-handed coldheartedness necessary to keep one's feet in the business world.

Genie had resisted comment, then and later. Maybe Mother Grant knew something he didn't. Maybe Philip, as a boy, had had a thing for dissecting rats or something; that sort of theory could be supported by the naked maliciousness in Philip's glare whenever he grew mad. But to Genie that was nothing more than a wildness he'd learned, after gaining the boy's trust, to exorcise casually with a promise that things would improve (that was something he'd learned long before: a little optimism, a reminder of the power of money could trivialize virtually any despair in the heart of a rich man). To Genie, Philip was no less spoiled and sybaritic than the rest of his family, and certainly no more cruel, for they were all cruel. Still, to Philip, Genie had been assigned, and, for ten years, it was to Philip that Genie had had to answer. If he'd habitually questioned, he would never have kept his job. He'd grown soft, and since Mother Grant's personal security forces had done most of the industrial espionage dirty work, Genie had ended up as little more than a complacent confidant—a "friend," as Philip often liked to say; when Philip had wakened him and sent him out to battle (granted, at the time, it was supposed to have been a straightforward recon mission), he'd gone off like an obedient puppy dog, giving it less thought than he would normally have given an assignment to escort Philip's sister, Rachel, to some-or-another vidaward ceremony.

Now, watching Philip, anger at himself began to bubble up through the memories. It had taken him the night's reflections to get it all into perspective, to realize how drastically the tides had turned, and how pathetic his pandering to the whims of the rich seemed in the starkness of a reality stripped bare of money. No amount of cash could turn back the tides now. How much brute, physical force would Mother Grant require to free her chosen heir now? Did she even know what had happened? Wherever the old witch was— he knew there was a second cryocomplex somewhere, probably within a hundred klicks—he was sure that she knew. Medusa would have seen to that. . . .

Philip was moving now, crawling, saying something in hushed tones to his cousin Martin. Genie almost laughed. What was there to talk about at this point? Jesus! he realized suddenly. *How had they ended up here, with him? Had the fools danced out into the night, all of them, or had these creatures—the owners of the eyes beyond the barbed wire —ripped a chunk from the earth and plucked them out? What the hell had happened after the battle?*

Still too many questions. Genie shrugged them off and crawled to the closest of his men. The boy—scarcely twenty, if Genie remembered correctly—was still out cold with a bruise the size a baseball along his lower left jaw. Gingerly, Genie placed his hand under the boy's head and felt his scalp, looking for fractures. Finding none, he laid the boy's head back, stroked his forehead, and moved on to the next man. This one hadn't been so lucky; around his legs, blood had pooled throughout the night. His face was white, and Genie made sure he could find a pulse before he tore open the man's pants around his wounded thigh. Blood still pumped lazily through a mass of dirt and scab, and Genie bent to the task of tearing a tourniquet from the torn trouser leg.

After a while, still so lost in his own thoughts that he failed to sense the approach, he heard Philip's voice behind him: "What are you doing?"

Words came slowly out of his silence, in the end like the lazy, scathing retort of a disturbed cobra. "What does it look like I'm doing?" he answered without turning.

"That man looks dead."

"He isn't." Genie finished tearing off the strip of cloth and began to tie it around the wounded man's upper thigh.

"You can't save him with that!" Philip said, impatiently trying to demand Genie's full attention.

"Used to work, Mr. Tyler-Grant," Genie said with cold formality. "You tie it off until you can stitch it up." He glanced back briefly, motioning for Philip to stoop down. "Even then, you have to loosen it every few minutes to let the blood circulate." He twisted the ends of the strip around themselves until the blood stopped pumping through the wound, then grabbed Philip's arm and forced the twisted knot into his hand. "If you don't, the wound festers and you end up chopping off the leg." He backed away and looked steadily into Philip's eyes.

"You've got to get us out of here, Genie!" Philip said, nervously tightening the knot.

"How?"

"I don't know! You're supposed to be the expert!"

"On what? You haven't even told me what year we're in."

"Six-thousand something—hell, I don't know—"

"Neither do I." He crawled to the next man, who was beginning to wake and attempting, feebly, to shade his eyes. "All I know is that lasers are definitely not the effective weapon in fashion this year."

"Shit!"

"Calm down, Mr. Philip. Tell you what: We'll go wherever you like. Shopping in the Village, maybe? A hop to L.A. to pick up the latest designer sportsflyer?"

"Damnit, Genie, I'm serious."

"So am I. Where do you expect to go? No—better yet, tell me how you got here. That's something that still puzzles me."

"Same as you. I got smashed by that black bastard, but I hit him with an antitank missile first."

"Did it do any good?"

Philip shook his head no.

"I suggest you reflect upon that fact for a moment."

Genie struggled to help the waking man sit. After a moment, Philip wordlessly threw down the tourniquet and stomped off, back toward his family. Genie glanced after him, then he guided the man who'd just wakened to where he could tend the wounded boy, and sat back, watching Philip's retreat.

Jan, Robert, Rachel—and the Morrisey-Grants, Andrew and Charlene, their son Martin, and his wife, Madonna— were all more or less awake now. Huddled off, in their own exclusive corner of the prison. Most of the mutants' attention had focused on the family; Genie wondered whether that was due to the presence of the women, or the simple fact that they fidgeted more, talked more, openly displaying their desperation.

Desperation . . . why couldn't he feel it? Could that be what his life had lacked all those years? He'd always thought of himself as a romantic in control. What if that was a contradiction in terms?

It was when Genie finally tore himself free of these thoughts that he first picked Algy out of the mutant crowd. A certain thoughtfulness suddenly revealed itself in the old one's gaze, in the way his eyes passively scanned over Philip and his family, rested lingeringly on Genie, and then moved back and forth between the two captive groups. While the other mutants were watching, like children in a zoo, the actions of the most colorful and interesting of their captive specimens, Algy observed all of them and seemed particularly concerned with Philip and Genie himself, as if he'd carefully observed Genie's earlier interaction with Philip and was waiting patiently to see what would happen next between them.

Genie watched Algy watching Philip, and he began to smile. When Algy's attention returned to him, he held his gaze steady and lifted his hand briefly in a muted gesture of greeting.

Algy simply stared his same, passive stare. Genie began to wonder whether he'd made some sort of horrible mistake, and the mutant's gaze seemed to grow heavier, more difficult to bear, with each passing second. Then, without warning, Algy's lips curled into a brief, enigmatic smile.

Just before he turned his attention back to Philip, the mutant winked.

VI.

For long moments, Tiffany did nothing but stare into her empty module. Her nightmare had come around in a circle; perhaps it had layered itself back upon itself. Here she was, dreaming herself back to where she dreamed. It still felt so real. Maybe she *had* wakened and wandered off to the cave with the stream and, there, had the dream of Stigg and Monk and the battle under the moonlight. Except she wore Stigg's robe, and she held his sun lantern in her hand. And where had that hole in the wall come from?

Medusa, she thought. "Medusa?" she asked aloud.

No answer.

No computer—she was supposed to be everywhere. Why didn't she work? Tiffany hadn't dreamed her any danger, so this must be some new twist of her nightmare. . . . What if the computers suddenly stopped? She'd probably heard that damned question over a hundred times during her lifetime. At least ten vids, from the absurd to the profound, had addressed the question, and only God knew how many science-fiction novels had taken it on. It was a question that four-year-olds asked their parents, and it was a question that always surfaced whenever party conversation descended to some "Oh, wow—heavy!" level. She'd gotten bored once at school and asked her instructionbot; some smart-ass had programmed the machine to recite the second and third verses of the fifth chapter of Revelation: *And I saw a strong angel proclaiming with a loud voice, Who is worthy to open the book, and to loose the seals thereof? And no man in heaven, nor in earth, neither under the earth, was able to open the book, neither to look thereon.* Whatever the hell that was supposed to mean—probably that she didn't understand the question she'd asked, couldn't understand it, and never would. Personally, she'd always thought the question a little absurd, so maybe she had understood it after all.

Now, however, she was confronted by it. Medusa didn't work—part of her nightmare? Had the computers finally stopped? No—that was getting totally carried away; she was a very capable programmer in her own right, and she understood the fact that any number of things could cause a software malfunction short of the sort of transmogrification of physics that the question suggested.

"Keep the logic tuned," she whispered softly, recalling a university catchphrase. In a dream? came her rhetorical, silent reply.

Stigg stopped by the river and scratched at the rock with his foot. Henna reached his side and looked down, puzzled. "What are you doing?" she asked.

"Tiffany's gone," said Stigg.

"She was here?"

"Yes. This is Stigg's secret river. Stigg left her here with his magic lantern to guard her from the dark creatures."

She stooped down, peering more closely at the rock. "What dark creatures? You've never mentioned them before."

Stigg chuckled. "They are funny! They make funny noises and try to bite Stigg. It tickles." He grew somber. "But Stigg saw Tiffany bleed when his pallet bit her. If Stigg's pallet can make Tiffany bleed, so can the dark creatures."

"She must have wandered off," Henna said, shining her own sun lantern around. "Where to?"

"She was dying," Stigg said distantly. "Maybe the dark creatures stole her from Stigg."

Henna reached up for his hand. "How? She had the magic candle to protect her, didn't she?"

Stigg nodded.

"Where could she have gone?"

"Anywhere," he said. He looked sadly down at Henna, then threw back his head. "Tiffany!" he cried out. "Where are you?"

The distant, echoing voice drew her attention away from the cryomodule. Stigg, she realized; she was no longer alone in her nightmare. She pictured him loping through the passageways, speeding her way, popping up suddenly into the chamber. . . . No, better not to think like that—nightmares could feed on those kinds of fears. Still, it was possible. And she needed to move on; she didn't feel comfortable staying where she was, there where her dream had shown her where she'd come from.

Cautiously, she tested the chamber's door. For a moment, she feared it wouldn't give; then the airtight seal popped softly, and she was through, pushing the door shut behind her, shining the sun lantern's beam around, and praying for no new surprises.

Philip's chamber.

Philip's cryomodule, open and empty, like her own . . .

Definitely a new twist: first Medusa, now Philip; further exploration would doubtless show her a whole host of empty modules. She'd thought earlier that she'd escaped her family; now the dream had turned and she'd learned the opposite: Her family had abandoned her.

So much for small favors, really. Philip's authoritarian ego was one thing she didn't need to cope with at the moment. And the last time she'd dreamed of him, she'd dreamed him emperor of some warped vision of ancient Rome. He'd sworn to her that his brother, uncles, and cousins plotted to kill him and take the throne that was rightfully his. That dream had had numerous chilling parallels to reality—her relatives definitely had their share of royal quirkiness, though they'd never descended, at least in her knowledge, to murdering their own—and she wasn't ready to deal with another like it. Philip had acquired certain paranoid qualities that Tiffany had found particularly troubling. She and Jan had tried to tell him that he'd taken to spending far too much time at his grandmother's feet, but they hadn't gotten through.

In the end, it had grown rather pathetic. Philip had pouted for an entire week after learning that he wouldn't be "hibernating," as some in the family had come to call it, in the same complex as his grandmother. It hadn't mattered that he would be nominally in charge of the second complex, or perhaps it had; perhaps that had been the source of his despair. Her brother might actually have been afraid of the responsibility. Tiffany had no problem seeing it in that light; Mother Grant expected too much from everybody.

Glancing back briefly at the empty cryomodule, Tiffany pushed through Philip's second door into the large, multi-purpose common area to which all the family's sleep chambers were attached. Here, dim, emergency lighting prevailed. Enough to see, but not enough to see clearly . . . Quickly, Tiffany went through the motions of verifying her abandonment. Robert's chamber was empty, so were Jan's and Rachel's and Martin's and Monica's. Looking into Jan's empty module, Tiffany began to cry. It was one thing to be relieved at the absence of her brother, but another entirely to find that her big sister had disappeared as well.

She didn't bother checking on Martin's parents. After finding her cousins absent, she collapsed to the floor next to Robert's door and thought how nice it would be to suddenly see Rachel's smiling face, even one of Madonna's childish fits. . . . Well, maybe not that—if she wished for it, it might come true, and then, surely, she'd regret it.

Eventually she forced herself to stand; the dream was going static, unchanging, silent, and forbidding like a dark, unknown beast readying to pounce. She turned out her attention, looking for hidden dangers.

Though she'd never liked it—from the first time she'd seen it, she'd thought it little more than a glorified bomb shelter—the common area had everything from an auto-kitchen to full-function recreational and entertainment systems. Not that any of it was likely to work without Medusa . . . The place was designed for long-term occupancy, and Tiffany suddenly remembered the trapdoor at the far end that led down to more rooms, real bedrooms and lounges, even a small gymnasium. If the others had wakened, they might have gone there. *Leaving her?*

Never mind, she thought, already moving across the room. She reached the trapdoor and knelt, then hesitantly pressed her palm to the access panel. The door opened upward, and a burst of musty air hit her in the face, as if the rooms below exhaled. The stairwell down was dark; she started to shine the lantern there, then paused. If there was no light (and she could hear no sound), then it was unlikely that anyone was down there. At least not anyone alive.

And if they'd gone there, and Medusa had later malfunctioned—well, the computer certainly had control over access to the complex's lower levels. The fact that the entrance security worked didn't mean that the exit security would. And a computer in its death throes could conceivably keep people trapped below. . . . Visions of a possibility— her family, all dead down in that darkness—came to her like a nightmare within the nightmare. She could go down and find skeletons, or perhaps signs that they'd eaten each other as the food supplies had dwindled. She could find them mummified, their ghosts clawing at her, drawing her into their hell of imprisonment, their agony, denying her escape even in their deaths.

No. . . . She chased the demons away. She couldn't go down; she couldn't risk trapping herself there, even if it was just a dream. Some phantom would have to push her in first. . . .

She jumped up and away, the thought of falling headfirst into the darkness still reeling through her mind. She looked about desperately: no phantoms, none that she could see, anyway. No one there at all; she tried to still the rapid beating of her heart, but the effort only intensified her alarm; it all felt too damned real!

Go exploring, Tiffany, she thought. *Move!*

She raced across to the autokitchen and wildly started punching buttons. Nothing worked!

"Medusa!"

She'd wanted it to be a shout, but it had emerged from her lips as scarcely a loud whisper. Still, it was almost deafening to her ears. Then something suddenly clanged inside the machinery, and she jumped back again, dropping into a defensive crouch. After a few moments, at the sound of a dropping cup, she stood to inspect the various, seemingly inert components of the autokitchen. As she did so, scenes of yet another vid came unbidden into her mind: *Death at Lunchtime* it was called, one of the wave of horvids that had been popular during her teenage years, this one about some maniac kitchen repairman who'd programmed his patients for murder. One of her friends had been stupid enough to buy the chip, and Tiffany had been stupid enough to let herself get talked into watching it.

Nothing so sinister here, she decided, determined to keep a grasp, however tenacious, on her reason. Just a cup of something and a chunk of something else in the *profibervit* generator, generic food, from an autonomous machine that probably drew power off the same source as the emergency lights. That would make good design sense; even without the main computer, humans stranded here could still see and eat and thus survive.

Actually, she thought uneasily, that makes too much sense. Logic, in a dream, was supposed to be the exception to the rule. She wondered if she should concentrate on Stigg and start opening doors, willing him, and all that other insanity, back into the nightmare. But that would probably just make things worse; she'd probably find working waste annihilators, toilets, and showers if she searched long enough.

Before her now, however, was food. The mere thought of it wakened loud growlings in her stomach, and, thankfully, that thought quickly chased all others away. Cautiously still, she approached the door of the *profibervit* machine and opened it. Tantalizing smells wafted out; she picked up the cup and sniffed at the liquid, then drank it in one long, luxurious gulp. The chicken-flavored protein cake went down as quickly, and she mashed down the machine's request button again, anxiously awaiting a second entrée.

When it came, she sat on the floor and ate more slowly, savoring each bite. Like everything else the Grant clan had ever bought, their *profibervit* generators were the best, masters of "modern tastes for modern tongues," or so claimed the vidverts.

As her hunger waned, she realized how strange it felt to dream of eating; she'd rarely done it in the past, and she'd never done it with generic food. But it tasted so *good*, as if she'd eaten nothing for thousands of years.

VII.

The stares were the worst.

Of that he was sure. It made him nervous; even when his sisters looked at him now, it made him nervous. Something had to happen, a change, an end to the stares, at least; they kept conjuring up his worst memories of childhood, like the time he'd forgotten all his lines halfway through a school production of *The Lion, the Witch, and the Wardrobe,* or the time he'd gone out with Alison Hemmings and attempted to roller-skate for the first and last time. He hated the mere memory of those experiences; they made him feel completely impotent, and whenever he thought of them, the nervousness and self-doubt would always superimpose themselves over the rest of his life, demanding recognition as aspects of his reality, stating firmly, by their presence, their fundamental claims on his true nature.

So he fled them, lashing out in defiance of the nagging voices within. Banish the stares, he thought. *Crush them!*

He was already on his feet, rushing at the staring eyes, but the metal stopped him. He clawed at the wires, biting them back with his hands until he could hold on and shake with all his fury. "Let us out of here!" he screamed. "We are not animals! Let us out of here!"

The stares only intensified, like worms, boring into his skull as if he were dead; he could almost feel them inside, eating his thoughts, devouring his flesh. Some of the faces smiled now; he screamed at them wordlessly, primally demanding they avert their eyes. And then something touched his shoulder. He spun, snarling.

"Calm down, Philip," Genie told him, his voice like a weak, unwelcome distortion in the hurricane of Philip's echoing screams.

Philip could *feel* the stares now, savagely piercing the back of his head. He glared at Genie a moment, then turned back, renewing his screams. This time the hand on his shoulder pulled him away from the wire, and he flew backward, landing jarringly on the stone.

Anger burned up his spine like crackling lightning, colliding with his mind in thunderous waves. He gained his feet again and rushed at Genie with flailing fists.

His target didn't move at all until he'd almost hit it, then Genie's arm became a blur and something smashed into Philip's jaw with terrible force. Again, he flew backward; again, he hit the stone, pain turning back the tides of anger, then bouncing around the inside of his head for a long time before subsiding.

In the pain's wake came a numbness, and into the numbness, the insecurities—the nervousness, self-doubts, and impotence—swiftly returned, chiding him for running, laughing at his failure, teasing him like a circle of chanting schoolchildren mocking his pride.

Philip Tyler-Grant kept his eyes closed and his head bowed. He drew his knees up to his chest, and he started to cry.

Genie stood silently, listening to the muffled sobs. The spoiled child within Philip had materialized so abruptly and without warning that he found it hard not to drop down next to the dirty, pathetic man and throw his arms around him the way a father might console a punished son. But the reality and tension of the situation quelled the paternal instinct; Genie had acted for Philip's sake, but he'd acted, also, for the sake of an audience. Philip's outburst had made many of their captors noticeably restless, and where before there had been simple curiosity, there now was some degree of confusion and, perhaps, even some fear. For all intents and purposes, Philip had directed his anger against a mountain, and that mountain was quite capable of reacting by collapsing down, unthinking, on all of them.

So Genie watched Philip a while, trying to be sure his victory would last a reasonable length of time. When he turned away, Algy stood directly opposite, on the other side of the wire. The old mutant eyed him thoughtfully, and Genie stood up straight, relaxing his shoulders and submitting to the gaze while he searched the old one's eyes. "Forgive him," Genie said softly, half to Algy, half to himself. "He doesn't understand."

"Neither do we," the old one answered.

Genie felt his eyes widen. He searched for more meaningful words but could find none. Confronted, unexpectedly, by perfect English, he'd found himself speechless.

VIII.

Tiffany listened at the door. When she'd reached it, it had been ajar; she'd almost stepped through, but a distant voice had stopped her.

Her negative selves had almost caught her; she knew it because she'd recognized the voice. Monk's voice.

For a few moments, she'd dared to peek through the crack into the hall beyond. The floor there was littered with cans, scraps of clothing, and assorted electronic equipment; she hadn't had long to wonder about it all before one of Monk's people—Fredo, if she remembered correctly—staggered into the hall under the weight of a huge crate.

She'd shut the door then; she could still hear them—sounds like shuffling footsteps up and down the hall. Occasionally she heard muffled voices, her negative selves, dismantling what was left of her family's heritage. . . . Had they taken Philip, Jan, Rachel, and the others as well? The door, when she'd found it, had been *open,* but she just couldn't imagine a mass abduction, not with the cryomodules behind her showing no signs at all of forced entry.

Padding softly back to the common area—it was only one long hall away—she realized that the various themes of her dream had suddenly converged, suggesting complications and implications they'd barely hinted at before. It would have overwhelmed her, but for the fact that she was still free, so the nightmare hadn't fully trapped her yet. Think, Tiffany! she thought. If her negative selves had breached the complex's security, Medusa might have tried to waken all of them. If they'd wakened, what might they have done? No safe place to hide on the main level—so they would have gone lower, right? And they would leave it dark and keep silent, cowering like trapped mice. She'd probably scared the hell out of them when she'd opened the trapdoor. . . . But why had they left her behind?

No, she thought, trying to correct her logic: Why had she dreamed that they'd left her behind? Was it simply her old doubts about her place among them? Did she secretly fear that they despised her because she was different, because she wouldn't mentally conform? Or was this one of those dreams in which she dreamed outside of herself, in which she would come, ultimately, to see herself as a character in her own vision? Her module had opened, just like the others. If she found them, she could find herself among them. And if she found herself, the dream would end, wouldn't it? How could it go on then? How could it then continue to feel so real?

The more she nurtured this hope, the more sure she felt about it.

* * *

Even with the sun lantern, she could find no dust on the steps leading down, no evidence of poor maintenance (which made Medusa's malfunction quite recent), but also no evidence of passage. The mystery refused to unravel.

She squatted, shining her light down to where the stairs ended in a landing, and the landing in a closed door. There was the rubicon, the borderline between dream and consciousness; beyond that door, she would wage battle for her mind, for her right to end this dream and move on to the next. The thought was transcendent; she felt as if the dream should accommodate her mood, clothe her in glittering armor, arm her with a shining, mystical sword. At the least it could make her glow a little, make her a creature of light descending to do battle with the forces of darkness. She tried to conjure a sword into her hand, but the dream refused. After a moment, she relaxed her hand and laughed softly. Here she was, trying to change the rules of the game: If the dream gave in now, then it would be admitting defeat even before the battle. No—she still had to accept *its* rules, lest it rob her of this one chance. The longer she hesitated, the longer her negative selves had to find her, to abduct her from this threshold of victory.

The threshold—the stairs—the rubicon that she must willfully cross. Beyond it she would confront herself, revealing the dream for all that it was. . . . She was hesitating now; it began to seem too simple. Was that because she was starting to doubt her earlier conviction, or was it some mental trick she played on herself to put off the confrontation? Was she coming to fear it because she understood the importance of victory, or was she fearing, instead, the possibility that she would find nothing below, that her abandonment had some other, more rational explanation within the boundaries of the dream's logic? And then would she find them there, dead in the darkness, as she'd first feared?

In the shadows now, wherever the lantern's beam did not shine, demons lurked. Tiffany stood up and shook her head, trying to fend off the tentacles of terror. She had toyed with the dream in asking for that sword, and the dream had retaliated swiftly, transforming her confidence (and her hope) into doubt and fear, trying to defeat her before the battle as surely as she'd idly attempted her own easy victory. The battle, she realized, had already begun.

She would not lose. She tried to remember she was still free, tried to keep that thought in the forefront of her mind. And as for the doubts—well, she would either find herself below with her family, or she wouldn't. If she did, she would fight the dream then and emerge victorious because she would be able to marshal all the forces of logic to her defense. If she didn't, then the dream would go on, but that didn't mean her defeat, no matter what she found below. And, she resolved defiantly, if the dream intended to trap her in the darkness, then it could go suck an egg. After all, her own subconscious was doing this to her, and there were limits to what she would take from anybody, even herself!

With that thought, and the beam of the sun lantern her only weapon, Tiffany tested the first step, then started down. When she cleared the entrance, the trapdoor hissed shut behind her. She paused, searching the walls of the stairwell for the panel that would hopefully let her open the trapdoor from this side. The only panels she could see were at the bottom; she had to go the rest of the way down. She swallowed, then hurried down the rest of the steps. On the landing, she found two hand-activated controls. The one next to the door, obviously, allowed access into the lower level; the other one, logically, should open the passage back up. . . . Slowly, she pressed her palm against the second. Above her, the trapdoor hissed open. She pressed the panel again, and the trapdoor closed. Smiling with renewed confidence, she readied the sun lantern for her plunge through the door.

She learned quickly, of course, that no one was there. In fact, only the grooved tracks of maintenance droids and the absence of dust suggested that anything at all had happened in the place since they'd sealed it off. And the lower complex had lights that worked the way lights were supposed to, coming on as she entered a room, going out as she left; the congeniality of the process made the task of verifying her solitude almost enjoyable.

She did find, however, more passages and rooms than she remembered, but she could attribute that to the fact that she'd paid little real attention to the briefings and tours that had preceded her entombment underground. At the time, the thought of being stuck in a claustrophobic community comprised solely of members of her family had seemed the worst of all possible futures, and she still couldn't blame herself for feeling that way. Because of this, exploring now suddenly became interesting. Apparently, even when her conscious mind couldn't have cared less, her subconscious mind had digested it all; either that, or it was rapidly filling in blanks—still a remarkable feat. It intrigued her, as if she'd stumbled haphazardly upon the mechanism of total recall. (Now, that would be a prize to emerge victorious with! Or would it? Did she really want to remember in detail everything, pleasant *and* unpleasant, that she experienced?)

Never mind, she thought, sliding into the console chair in one of the newly discovered control rooms. The chair's tension correctors buzzed on, expertly and rapidly sending soothing waves of ecstasy up and down her body, unknotting every small muscle, relieving aches she'd not noticed she'd had until they were gone. And her eyes—closed now, with a dreamy mirage of a sunset sky floating in and out, up and down. . . .

Part of her wanted her to open her eyes, to test the console; if the chair worked, shouldn't the computer? It wouldn't be Medusa in all her glory, but it could easily be a subset; they'd all had subsets of Medusa in their flyers, back in the old days. . . . If she could talk to it, hear a voice in her own language. . . .

But she was winning now; the dream was going away. And she was back on the beach, lazily soaking up the last rays of the dying sun.

Gulls screamed overhead; she scratched idly in the sand—a comic face. When she finished it, she rose up to her elbows and smiled; then she recognized Stigg's features staring back up at her, and she quickly brushed them away.

Her heartbeat quickened as she waded out into the waves, embracing both ocean and sky with open arms, praying to them, silently, to keep her safe.

IX.

"English?" Philip asked. "What did he say?"

"Nothing much," Genie said. "I'm going out. He invited me."

Philip's eyes flickered with a disturbing fire. "Then you can get us out of here. Escape. Get to Mother Grant—she'll do the rest."

Genie eyed him calmly. "First of all, no. I don't know where she's at, and even if I did, I wouldn't dare it. Besides, if she cares, she'll already know, but why do you suppose she'll do any better than you did? Since she isn't as stupid as you are, she may decide to do nothing at all, leave you here to fend for yourself. That's what you deserve, anyway."

The fire in Philip's eyes grew darker. "I'll get you, you bastard."

"Sure you will."

"I'm going with you," Martin Morrisey-Grant said.

"Like hell!" Genie said, turning on him. "We're all in this now, and I'm not taking orders from any of you anymore. You can do what I say or go fuck yourselves for all I care! But you do anything stupid and you'll get the same thing he got," Genie finished, pointing at Philip.

Martin stared at him; Genie watched the anger growing in his eyes and chuckled. "You two just don't understand, do you? We can't afford to make mistakes, can't afford to be stupid. Algy asked for me, and that's who he's going to get. Consider yourselves lucky, goddamnit! We can *talk* to them! They can just as easily kill us, and if you two keep up with this bullshit, they probably will. If you had any sense you'd listen to me!"

"Damnit, Genie," Philip protested. "You act like this is all our fault! Tiffany started it! Where the hell is she, anyway?"

"I don't know. Maybe I can find out if you'll give me a chance."

"Stop blaming Tiff," Jan interjected wearily. Genie smiled at her, grateful for the support. She was a strong, compassionate woman; until now, she'd sat quietly with one arm around Rachel (who kept her face hidden in Jan's shoulder) and the other around Robert (who looked on, a passive, unreadable smile pasted on his face).

"Shut the fuck up, Jan," Philip said.

"You shut the fuck up yourself. For all we know, Tiffany's dead! Your sister, Philip!"

Genie watched them, trying not to smile, trying to keep a good grasp on the gravity of the situation. But Jan handled her brother remarkably well. . . . As for the rest of them,

Martin had retreated on his own; his wife, Madonna, had joined him, her shoulders slumped and head bowed, as if she wanted to hold him but was afraid to make the first move, afraid that even a display of tenderness might redirect his anger toward her. The remaining Grants, Andrew and Charlene Morrisey-Grant, Martin's parents, sat to one side, huddled together against the wall, staring blankly at nobody in particular.

"Please," Genie said at last. "All of you—be quiet. We're being watched. We're also being heard. Don't you realize? At least one of them knows English!"

Philip still glared at him, but he said nothing else. After a moment, Jan looked at Genie and smiled wanly. "You're right," she said. "Go. We'll wait, as patiently as we can."

Algy took Genie directly to his lab. They passed, on the way, a small mound of crates that Genie immediately recognized as a significant fraction of the Tyler-Grant supplies. On the horizon, he noticed two figures approaching, both balancing impossibly heavy loads on their shoulders and looking, in silhouette, something like bizarre, blockheaded aliens. More had been happening, he realized, than he'd guessed at.

During the brief journey, he saw much of the community and surrounding area. He noted the haphazard constructions, some obviously inhabited, some abandoned. He passed several small, irrigated fields where the mutants grew the mineral compounds and crystals that provided them sustenance. The sight only puzzled Genie at the time; he could imagine no purpose for the rows of wet, shiny rock. Beyond those fields, stalks of strange plants that bore cornlike husks rose up from the ground; Genie had no way of knowing that the more traditional vegetation grew for nothing but to feed Algy's still.

At least they had water, from a spring or a well or something. Genie grew thirsty just looking at it and smelling it in the air.

The building they eventually reached, Algy's lab—Genie felt he could lose himself in it for days. He'd entered a nostalgist's paradise: everything from clocks to radarpoles, Coke bottles to guitars to a polished, reconstructed, vintage 2031 Camairo (It must've come in piece by piece, he thought. Have to tear down a wall to get it back outside. . . .) In one corner was a stack of oil paintings, the one in front looking suspiciously like an authentic Picasso. That wasn't all that surprising, he realized, since only museums traditionally went to extremes to protect the greatest works of art from the ravages of war. Most of the world's mediocre oils would have gone up in flames along with the walls they'd hung on.

Algy, silent during their walk, let Genie wander freely through his collection. He didn't speak until Genie hesitantly reached out to touch the flyer.

"I never could make it fly," Algy said. "I tried but failed. There's so much I still don't understand."

"About what?"

"Everything. All this," he said, waving his arm around. "Pieces of the past that I collect. Why these things were; how they came to be."

"Flyers," Genie said. "Once, the skies were full of them."

"Why?"

"Because people couldn't move around on the ground very well anymore. There were too many people, so the ones who had money flew to wherever they wanted to go to get there faster."

Algy walked up behind Genie. "I still don't understand. I've seen many old picture stories with flyers in them, and

I once thought I understood until I realized that the stories weren't really true, just make-believe. Were there galactic empires? No—just empty space up there filled with fantasies. Were there really great wars, nations of millions . . . Russia and America, Germany and Japan?"

"That much was true."

"But what truths do I know about them? Which picture stories do I believe? Did people really grow old and die, and did their children grow up like them, and do the same?"

Genie turned to him, puzzled. "Yes. You don't? You, of all I have seen, look aged."

"I have looked as I do since I can remember. I have never known anyone to grow old and die."

"Your children?"

"We—we have no children."

Algy looked away, walked away from the flyer. Genie felt tension worming its way into the conversation like an unwelcome guest. Had the old one lied? About himself or the children? Or was it something else—some eternal agony known to his host that Genie couldn't begin to understand? Then again, how could Genie be sure he'd perceived anything correctly? The entire conversation seemed, in retrospect, to have emerged abruptly from the soil of the night's reflections; was he coping, talking now with an immortal descendant of humanity who'd apparently learned of the past through vidtechnology that had survived mankind itself? Could the tension be his alone? No, something in their words had touched Algy, perhaps something as simple and basic as the concept of death. Genie still knew nothing of the extent of the casualties he and his men had inflicted before their defeat, but to ask it now—no, why widen the rift or deepen the chasm of pain? He would learn; he had gained trust and would do or say nothing now to lose it. If he could help it.

"Perhaps," Genie said, stepping back from the flyer,

"you may yet see it airborne. My men were well trained, and one or two among them are fair mechanics."

"That will be up to Monk," Algy said, still distant. "In the end, much of this will be up to Monk; he is the vessel of all our pains, our joys and sadnesses, life and death. He is our only son."

Monk? Genie wondered. The big black one? The leader? "What will he do?"

"I don't know. He grew enraged last night; perhaps he remains that way." Algy turned to face him. "What shall we do with you? Shall we keep you caged, free you, even let you live? These questions only Monk can answer. Why did you attack us? Why did you kill Bobo? Why did you *want* to kill?"

Genie lowered his eyes. "We—I didn't."

"But you tried!"

"It was my job," Genie said softly, forcing himself to look up into Algy's eyes. "I was a warrior. Warriors kill."

"Willfully?"

"Mechanically. Like the sun rises and the rains rain. I knew nothing; I didn't think. I just did as I was told, and I was told to do my job."

"Told by whom? The man you argued with earlier?"

Slowly, Genie nodded.

"He is not a pleasant man? He wanted you to kill us?"

Genie thought of Philip, crying there in the dirt. "He didn't understand, either."

"He still doesn't understand," Algy said emphatically. He walked back to the flyer and touched it thoughtfully. "You are truly from the past."

Genie didn't immediately answer, because Algy didn't phrase it as a question. As a statement, the old one's words seemed to condemn, to sentence with their finality. Yes, Genie thought, *from the past. We stink of it, don't we? Our presence here is the sole malignant blemish in your oth-*

erwise perfect, eternal Earth. We destroyed it once, and you must blame us; for who else might you blame? Here, now, our disease may spread again. . . . Perhaps you understand that we are the disease; perhaps you must kill us. Perhaps you have no other choice.

"To us," Genie said at last, "you are from the future. You are the end of that which we began, the result of a world out of control. Your presence changes our world, a world we hoped to keep by waiting for this time—this future, but you've stolen it from us, don't you see? This is your world now, not ours. And we are at your mercy."

"How did you get here?"

"We slept. We slept and let the years go by, hoping to escape the madness of the end of our world. Many of us could see it coming, but we were powerless to stop it. Did you learn that much about us from the vid?"

"The picture stories? Yes."

"The worst thing of all is that we wakened now by mistake. Or by tragedy, or fate, I don't know. We wouldn't have attacked you, and you might never have known us, but for Tiffany. We only tried to find her and bring her back among us, but you found her first."

Algy remained silent for a long while. When at last he spoke, his voice was coarse and mournful. "Stigg found her," he said. "Stigg found her, we welcomed her, and then Bobo died. She did not say she was lost."

"Where is she now?"

"With Stigg, I hope. Henna should have brought them up by now; I begin to fear that something else horrible might have happened."

"I don't understand."

Algy tried to smile. "Don't worry. If we can, we'll return your Tiffany to you. After that, Monk will have to decide. I must take you back to your people now; I must think on what I have learned from you."

"And I from you. But we must have water and food, Algy. Can you get us that much?"

"Water, yes. But food—you eat living things, do you not? Animals, and green things that grow from the ground?"

"Uh—I guess so."

"I fear that our normal food is not right for you. I know a place, though, where things *do* grow. I will send some friends to gather some, but it will take time. We do not go to this place often."

"What of the green things we passed on our way here? They might do."

"That is not for eating," Algy said. "That is for firewater."

"For what?"

"Firewater. Whiskey, gin, Smirnov, whatever you called it."

Genie chuckled. "You drink *liquor?* We may have something in common after all."

Algy eyed him curiously for a moment; then the mutant, too, began to laugh.

X.

A tanned hand reached down out of the golden sky, and she reached up for it and squeezed it as it pulled her up and out of the water. As she rose, the sea clung to her, a forsaken lover, its watery arms raking mournfully down her skin like giant tears.

And then she stood before him; he could be God, she thought, with his eternal sky-blue eyes and the way he had ended her endless memory of swimming. He stood there, gazing at her with a silent smile, his hand still lightly holding hers.

Under her feet, the warm deck of the yacht moved lazily over the waves. Looking down, her feet were fins. She looked at *him* again, at his eyes, his curly golden hair, his bronzed skin. He had stolen her from her lover; as she'd swum, the sea had whispered in her ear ancient secrets of its majesty, its power and pain, the pain of its guardians, the whales who sang its harmonies and could tease melody from sadness and rhythm from death. The whales had died; the sea had shown her the vision. She'd cried and promised to sing its songs, but he had rescued her.

Who was he? Would he love her now? The sky was in his eyes, but so was water. . . . Would he let her sing her songs? Was he the sea itself, or was he God?

Again, gulls screaming. Where were they? She could only see the sky through his eyes. So blue, those eyes. Blue eyes . . . everything around them began to grow dark, even his skin, like a statue. . . .

He reached for her breast, touched her, and she knew him. He had not saved her; he was the *other* dream. She turned from him and began to run, the deck stretching out to the horizon before her, like a giant bridge across the ocean. She screamed, and the deck fell away, but she didn't fall into the water. She fell into a chair.

The other dream had her again, and it called to her: *"Complex Two, do you read? Complex two—damnit, Philip or whoever you are, answer me! Complex Two . . ."*

Like a chant. She opened her eyes and found the source of the voice, a speaker in the comm-bank. "Medusa," she said groggily, "acknowledge."

The console lights activated at once, a chorus of red, greens, blues, and yellows.

"Basic functions operative, Tiffany. . . . Expert functions loading. . . . Incoming radio-comm, voice ident positive, your father, Elison Grant. Do you wish to answer? . . . Fully functional, overrides acknowledged, and establishing visual contact. Transferring control. . . . Answer your father, Tiffany.''

The vidscreen in the comm-bank cleared, revealing a worried, middle-aged face that quickly grew red with anger.

"Tiffany! What the hell is going on there? Where's your brother? What the hell have you been doing, sleeping? Wake up, damnit! Why the hell did it take you so long to reactivate Medusa? Never mind—Medusa! Transmit status report!''

"Raw data transmission is under way, Mr. Grant. Preliminary analysis indicates that a programmed termination was initiated within the security subsystem due to violations of rules one, two, seventeen, and twenty-five of the security protocol list.''

"Speak English!''

"Physical intrusion into the complex, Mr. Grant, by unidentified individuals displaying hostile behavior in the absence of adequate resistance and the absence of an override command to remain functional. My main complex systems remain inoperative under the original directive of the security subsystem. In other words, all rules remain broken.''

"They're still up there?''

"Yes, Mr. Grant.''

"Get them the hell out!''

"How, Mr. Grant? Since all available forms of active resistance have proven futile, I am directed to download critical systems and data and engage in passive resistance in order to protect my hardware.''

"Damnit, Tiffany! What the hell is she talking about?''

"I—don't know. I mean, I'm not sure I understand all of it.'' She could have said more, but the idea made her feel ill. She'd already, somehow, let her father into the dream. If she dragged him in all the way, she would lose control, lose her freedom. . . .

"Where's your brother?''

"Jesus, Dad! I don't know!''

"You don't *know*!"

"Stop shouting, Dad. Please!"

"Medusa! Where's Philip?"

"I don't know, Mr. Grant. He isn't here."

"Tiffany!"

"Medusa," Tiffany pleaded, "can you at least turn him down?"

"I'm sorry, Tiffany, but your father has overriden your authority."

That was her problem. . . . *Think, Tiffany!* Her father hadn't stopped yelling at her; she was trying to shut him out. "Medusa," she asked desperately, "what is my authority?"

"Level eight, local."

"And my father's?"

". . . answer me!"

"Relative to local?"

"Yes!"

"Level three."

"Tiffany, damn you!"

"Philip's?"

"Level two, local."

"Philip's not here. Have you adjusted local authorization levels accordingly?"

"That task must be voice-initiated."

"Do I have the authority?"

"Tiffany!"

"Yes."

"Then adjust local authorization levels."

"Working, Tiffany."

"Answer me, young lady! I know what you're trying to do, and if I have to get your grandmother to make you listen, your ass—"

"Levels adjusted, Tiffany."

"—is mine!"

"What's my authority?"

"Level two, local."

"Tiffany!"

"Kill transmission, Medusa!"

Abruptly, the vidscreen went blank. Tiffany let out a slow sigh and eased back into the console chair. The tension correctors quickly relaxed her, and she felt a broad smile spreading over her face. She'd won again! Her father had tried to force himself into her dream, but she'd outsmarted him, and she'd pushed him out.

But Mother Grant . . . her grandmother. He'd said he would get her! What if . . . ?

Don't think about it, Tiffany! Don't make it happen!

She couldn't not think about it. Mother Grant's stern features began to fill her thoughts. Tiffany remembered how even her father would transform into a wimpering idiot faced with the old woman's wrath. She remembered a time— she'd been only a little girl—when her grandmother had crushed one of her dolls (her favorite doll!) under a spiked high heel and then laughed. . . . *"This is you, little Tiffany, if you grow up with a soft heart. . . ."*

So what if Mother Grant invaded her dream now and took control? Tiffany looked up at the ceiling and grew afraid as she imagined that huge spiked heel breaking through, coming down at her head.

"Medusa, I've got to leave," she said.

On her way out, she stopped briefly by her room—the room long ago designed to be her bedroom—and grabbed a pair of synth-denim jeans, a few shirts, a jacket, and a pair of boots. She didn't stop long enough to dress until she'd gone up through the trapdoor.

There, everything was quiet. Medusa still wouldn't respond, and she had time to breathe. But not much time— Monk and his people could come her way at any moment.

Everybody chased her now. At least her family hadn't abandoned her; well, her father hadn't, anyway. Seeing him—hearing him—she understood again why she'd always wanted to get away. She'd always *had* to get away.

She was free now. . . .

She went to autokitchen and punched the *profibervit*'s buttons until she'd filled a bundled shirt with protein cakes; then, armed with Stigg's sun lantern, she went back through her cryochamber into the tunnels beyond.

XI.

Rachel drained her third cup of water and went back to the bucket for another. Before sitting, she offered the cup to Philip, who shook his head, swearing under his breath that he'd die of thirst first.

"You'll die of something, Philip," Jan told him. "Drink, damnit!"

"No!" He looked up and glared at her. "For all we know, it's poison!"

"It's water, brother," Rachel said, taking a drink, then raising her cup and nodding at those who watched them.

"What the hell are you doing!" Philip yelled at her.

"I'm thanking them," she replied, turning on him. "They could just let us die in here, you know? Maybe we'll get the food Genie promised next."

"I won't eat it!"

"Yes, you will," Jan insisted. "Even if you are an asshole, you'll eat it when you smell it."

He glared at her but said nothing, and all fell silent until one of Genie's men brought over a fresh bucket of water and took the old away. With water still lapping over the sides and down into the dirt, Martin Morrisey-Grant rose, took the cup from Rachel, filled it, drank it, and filled it again.

"Not you, too, Martin!" Philip moaned.

"Gotta live to fight, Phil," his cousin said, handing the cup to his wife, who had yet to speak a word in the presence of the water. She drank, smiling meekly at her husband. Martin then filled the cup again and pushed it into Philip's face. "Drink it! It's only water—remember what water tastes like? Cool, wet . . ."

Philip started to push the cup away; then he grabbed it, threw his head back, and poured its contents down his throat. "There," he said to Martin. "Satisfied?"

"Yes."

"That's a good boy, Phillie," Jan said, laughing. "But you won't get dessert until you finish your veggies!"

"Shut up! You're all going to get it for this!"

"For what?" Jan argued. "For ordering an attack on the natives and getting the cryocomplex blown wide open in the process?"

"It was Tiffany's fault!"

"That remains to be seen." Jan spoke sadly, letting her words trail off into resignation, the mention of Tiffany shifting the focus of everyone's thoughts. Rachel moved close to her again, resting her head on her shoulder.

"I'm scared, Jan," Rachel whispered softly. "What if Tiffany's hurt, or worse?"

"She's okay," Jan said, hoping the assurance would dispel her own fears. "Tiff's a big girl; she can take care of herself."

The conversation, then, dropped off into silence, leaving all to sift through private thoughts, private memories, each seeking a way to deal with the unexpected, but undeniable, reality at hand.

Meanwhile, the eyes of their watchers never strayed.

* * *

Genie spent the afternoon away from the Tyler-Grants. He'd told them, upon his return, of the meeting with Algy, some of what he'd seen and heard, but mostly that they had to remain calm and not alarm their captors. "Wait for Tiffany," he'd told them. "They promised to find her and bring her back."

Where was she?

He wished he could have told them he knew. . . . At any rate, he didn't talk with them long, but left them to themselves while resolving to keep a wary watch from a distance. He would not allow Philip another outburst if he could help it. At the same time, he felt a need to maintain the separation between himself and Philip that had opened the door for a rapport between himself and Algy; they couldn't risk losing that. No matter what happened, no matter what, *"Monk would decide."* . . .

He definitely hadn't told the Tyler-Grants that part of Algy's words; the image in his own mind was too ominous, too unsure. Monk remained an unknown quantity—why terrify them with uncertainty? No better way to encourage Philip to go off the handle again.

No, he'd just told them the safe parts: about the water and food and the hopes that Tiffany would soon come back. He would have to shoulder the burden of doubt on his own.

Besides, he had his men to attend to. They needed explanations and understanding; they also were afraid and, as such, just as likely to cause problems. Of course, most had endured hardships in the past, which gave them something of an advantage. Still, friends of theirs had actually died the night before. Sentiment, while he was away, had turned against Philip; it was half Genie's fault—in a hurry, he'd told his lieutenant, Adrian, to restrain Philip at all costs if it became necessary. The result had brought a natural animosity to the surface, with Genie's men remaining apart from their employers and watching them with hawk-eyed vigilance, like slaves to whom rebellion had suddenly become conceivable.

In a way, the situation had helped his men, for though they certainly felt captive, for a while they had also had some feeling of control. Peace had been kept, but damage had also been done; already mutinous remarks could be heard openly, if half-jokingly, among the ranks. One man even suggested they abduct Rachel and "take turns tasting the fruit of high society." In spite of the man's rather poetic turn of phrase, Genie had slapped him down, telling him that this was no time for "adolescent fuck fantasies" and that "any shit-for-brains under my command will lose it if he pulls it out for anything but to piss."

He'd hated the words coming out of his mouth, even as he'd said them. Still, men were men, though those he commanded had generally outgrown the need for a drill sergeant. At the same time, in a way, he really couldn't blame the kid. What did any of them have to live for now? Even if the mutants set them free?

As the day settled into a silence of resigned anticipation, Genie found his thoughts turning back to Crystal, to that last afternoon . . .

. . . even if he got out of this, he could never get her back.

XII.

The passageways had a sort of peaceful, enchanting quality; they were wide, often opening up into small caverns, where she would find a stalactite here, a glittering wall there. She wondered at the forces that must have formed them. Ancient rivers? Volcanic gases from the depths of the Earth?

Just her dreams, she remembered. They could be any kind of caves she could wish them to be. She was winning now; she'd thrown her father out and escaped again. She had clothes and food. Now, could she twist the caves to her own will? To go wherever she might dream, a fantasy land of eleven princes, wine, dance, and song, a dream of Eden with pear trees and golden apples and the man she'd always dreamed of, the one with whom she could start the human race anew. Then the fruit of her womb would go out, over the land, to live and die. . . . Somewhere above, the Carpenter and His angels would take up their hammers and, in heaven, a new subdivision would be born to house the souls of this, her new race.

Well, it was a thought. The image of Jesus slaving, hammer in hand, made her giggle until the sound came back, echoing, to her ears. Quiet, she thought. Who knew where enemies might lurk? What secrets lie in the dark corners of the Earth. . . .

Rock, shaped like a pedestal. It made her feel she'd discovered some primal cathedral, the place, perhaps, where the bats came to pray. . . . She could hear them now and then in the distance. At least she *hoped* they were bats. Occasionally, the chitterings had sent chills up her spine; sometimes she'd felt them very near, but she'd yet to shine her light on even a hint of movement.

She stopped to eat there, at the pedestal, laying out her *profibervit* cakes in mock ceremony, imagining a cadre of waiters hidden just beneath the surface of the rock wall before her. And, as she ate, she felt the warm breeze. At first she thought it an errant draft, but it persisted, growing even stronger, and it brought with it strange scents, like flowers or blossoms. Like a garden; she smiled—*her Eden?* Had she willed it into her dream? Could she as easily summon her waiters into the cavern? Transform her meal into something real, naturally organic? No, it didn't work; she couldn't quite concentrate on it, though; the scents had grown too mysterious, too tantalizing. They evoked memories of forgotten afternoons among trees and flowers, a blanket, a stack of vidzines, and an ice-packed canister of banana daiquiries. . . . When she'd dreamed of knowing Hollywood present and Hollywood past, before Rachel had almost given it to her, before Mother Grant and the cryo-complexes had taken it away, taken it all away—the whole world. *Damn them!* she thought. They could have let her try to stay! Better to die than spend centuries fighting dreams. . . .

The air grew more fresh, more vital, with each step; the passageway she took led ever upward, toward her Eden. She was sure it was there now; the smells were real (real in her dream), the breeze was real (like the gentle warmth of those moments at the edge of sleep), and the joy in her heart—it was real as well.

So she doubted nothing, questioned nothing, when the sunlight devoured the beam of her lantern and she emerged from the Earth's embrace into her Eden, the place Stigg knew as the danger place, the *greenplace* Monk's people both worshiped and feared, the place to which Algy had earlier sent several of his people to collect food, of a sort, for Genie and the Tyler-Grants.

Had Algy known more—learned more from Genie—he might have thought longer on the problem of feeding Genie and his people. To the mutants, the food that grew in Tiffany's Eden meant madness, a madness they nevertheless inflicted upon themselves from time to time, but a madness, also, that needed a definite end, that needed to be returned from. They did not eat, then, from Eden often.

Algy had assumed, long before, that the eating habits of the ancients told him one of two possible things: The ancients were immune to the madness of their food, or the madness of the food had caused the madnesses of the ancients. Though he tended to believe in the latter, neither of these ideas was true, but Algy had found little to cause suspicion over the years. He'd known that the *greenplace* was unique, but he hadn't known just how unique it was.

Tiffany, of course, didn't even think about it. It was, after all, something she'd dreamed for herself. The fact that she'd found it, summoned it up in the midst of a dream of a barren world of infertile land and caves, only reinforced the illusion that she was, in truth, dreaming. And when one is convinced that experience is dream, something happens in the mind and imagination is suddenly relieved of the burden of acknowledging reality, and it can, at times, fly free, like a bird.

For this reason, as Tiffany danced through the springs of her garden, gravitating with uncanny instinct toward Eden's center, she heard music in her mind. The music was real, perhaps more real than anything else she perceived because it was contained completely within her mind though she felt that it came from the air. It had volume and texture, and subtlety and movement, drama and tragedy. It started as a single harp, then grew into an orchestra, into an eclectic symphony that took her breath away with its beauty. In its way, the music was a personal, poetic reaction to this, her dream of Eden. And it filled her, lifting her arms high, sending her whirling like a ballerina over the grass.

Later, when in a quiet moment she recalled some pale ghost of that orchestra in her mind, she wondered at the hidden power within herself, the force she'd experienced that she knew must have flowed freely through those gifted composers of the past. Within how many did this power lie hidden, untapped, fated never to emerge? Were reality's chains so unforgiving?

From time to time after that, she tried willfully to call the music forth again. Always she failed, and with failure, she cried, understanding that a loss of beauty is far more painful, far more real, than beauty never found.

XIII.

Henna went with five others to bring back food for the ancients. Algy sent her on this mission after she told him that she and Stigg had not yet found Tiffany.

Henna had left Stigg after they'd gone back to his home for his map. She'd grown depressed there, underground in the darkness; Stigg's tunnels always seemed to do that to her. Now she wished she'd stayed with him; the thought of going to the *greenplace,* even with others, even if she wasn't going to eat, made her tremble. She wasn't sure why she felt that way, but that didn't make her fear any less real. To Henna, the danger place meant power. It meant birth—the birth of her people. She, being one who could remember, knew they had all once lived there. Until they'd learned to leave and make the nightmares go away.

But only in that place had her people ever conceived.

Only there had she given birth, even though her babies had never survived. She remembered when Karmen gave birth to Monk and how happy they'd all been to see a child live and grow. But he'd been the only one, and Karmen the only mother.

All other mothers knew only death. And now Karmen was blind.

Next to Fredo, Henna ran across the land, attempting to find a thoughtless refuge in the rhythm of her stride. It didn't work; her thoughts were too powerful. She thought of the place they sought, its peaceful facade, its memories and its horrific treachery.

When they came in sight of it, she wished she could be like Stigg, simple, uncomprehending.

When they reached it and began gathering the food, she kept her eyes on the ground, intent on her task. She refused to look around.

The others with her, she sensed, did the same.

XIV.

Tiffany watched them.

Their noises had chased the music away, and she'd crept toward them and peeked carefully down, through the bushes.

More of Monk's people. She'd almost run from them before she'd realized that they weren't searching for her; they had come to pick mushrooms and other fruits of her Eden.

Let them go on, she thought. Now that she controlled the dream, she could be generous with it, share it with others—her negative selves. Perhaps then they would leave her alone, granting her a respite she might use at last to break the dream's repetitive grip. Or did she want that now? Now that she controlled? What if the next dream were more nightmarish and more real than the worst parts of this one?

Silently she watched them until they left; then she turned back into the heart of the garden.

At the nearest spring, she stooped to drink. As she rose, the colors around her seemed to grow more vivid; the greens of the leaves pulsated against the blue above, and little flowers, red and white and violet, winked brightly at her from atop their stems among the rippling grass. Like minarets, she thought, listening to the wind for her music's return.

And it came, a dark, mournful wailing that made her think of disembodied spirits, of heartbreak, the sadnesses of war, and of peace. Between herself and the nearest trees, an image of a cadre of blook-soaked, limping soldiers sprang up. Their eyes transfixed her with their hollow emptiness, that vacant gaze no longer capable even of pleading for an end. Abject surrender to violent death—they could have been any warriors who had ever fought, victims of some generic war. Then, bursting through the line of soldiers, came Oedipus, his eyes bloody holes, his screams mingling with the wail, the two sounds like dueling serpents, twisting, caressing with melody, fanging with dissonance, poisoning each other, dying together.

The vision faded with the music, and Tiffany found herself on the ground, in the grass, blinking her eyes against the deep brightness of the blue overhead. Like a trip, she thought. For a moment it had felt just like a trip.

But it was a dream, she told herself. Trips felt like dreams, not the other way around. Maybe this one was dissolving.

Something in the Earth moved, she thought. She could see it in the way the grass rippled and bucked. Around her but not underneath her. Eden was trees and bushes, grass and flowers, water and sky. The sky reached down and the water reached up in misty pillars to feed the high clouds;

the music of the molecules (she could hear it, high and tinkling, like snowflakes striking a windowpane) streaked across the heavens to die in the distant desert.

Desert winds—hot, barren, and proud—sang back.

She closed her eyes, and the music came down in a waterfall of evanescent blues and greens. In the surf floated faces shrouded in tears. Her tears, cried a thousand times, a thousand years ago. They *could* be hers—water was eternal.

Dream split dream. Sometimes it was melodic, the strands of the new infiltrating the old with the grace of dancers' arms, which grew into legs, then pillars, then whirling towers of color that suddenly stopped, like some fantastic slot machine, on a picture of a fiery-eyed swan or a man with legs where his arms belonged while tentacles grew out of his hips. At other times the new vision simply exploded into the old, ripping it away from her eyes as if it were but a balloon image of reality that could be deflated, its three dimensions folding into two, then one, then into nothing at all.

Nothing at all. She began to pray for it when the deflated reality-balloons fought back, jostling for center stage, the images they bore distorted and grotesque. Some when she screamed, but the sound of that, too, melted in her ears, becoming honey, then a wine that soured and filled the air with a stench of vinegar that hovered over her to do battle with the balloons and the color wheels.

Dreams within dreams. She was, after all, Eve, and as mother of Man she knew all. She knew the trees and the flowers and the springs that fed the clouds. She knew all the secrets—how her children had flourished and loved and learned war and then taken it to the stars. She knew the Answers.

She sat on Chronos's lap as he ate his children and spat them out again onto the fields of Earth.

She watched the cats come down from the sky in their silver ships, and she smiled as they trained men to build their temples, the pyramids they required to preserve their bodies while their spirits traveled back out to the stars.

And the rest of her children—she watched them make gods of ghost stories and ghost stories of gods. The true spirits fled back into the earth where only a few, with drum and incantation, could find them.

Socrates knew. She'd liked him until he'd started to believe in his own mythology of man, poisoning history in the process. They'd sent the Nazarene, of course, but he'd only made things worse. Too much blood. It might have worked if He'd come before Aristotle. Stoics and clerics threw the entire creation out of whack; man was much too weak for those standards. Later, some real ideals began to surface, but Copernicus was persecuted, Galileo recanted, and by the time they caught on, nobody was listening. Even then, Leonardo almost managed it; he gave them something they could understand while not understanding. He gave them a smile—his smile, her smile—the smile that *knew*.

And then they'd burned it with the rest of Paris.

In Utopia they held councils; she knew it was absurd, for what was there to decide? All there should know the truth, so why talk? Even Utopia was imperfect.

At the councils she discovered a word, and within the word, comfort. The word could not be said, neither could it be thought. She could only imagine it, cherish it, and nourish it as if it were the most precious child born to woman. To think it would damage it; to speak it would destroy it entirely. She discovered it, marveled at it, kept it near her heart, and walked away.

At Utopia's gates, the gatekeeper challenged her. "I have a word," she told him, and walked out. They gathered on the wall and watched her, all envious of her freedom, all too proud to speak their envy.

In the desert, the word fed her and quenched her thirst.

On the sea, the word kept her afloat, and it kept the sun's heat off her skin.

In the forest, she found a child. The child was blind and afraid. Before the word, she'd been a healer. She touched the child's eyes, but the child remained blind. She spoke to it softly, but it did not hear. In desperation, she called up the word. She tried to think it, but it eluded her. She tried to say it, and pain stabbed at her heart. The word remained silent.

She touched the child, and the child fell, dead, to the ground.

She still had the word. She could still *imagine* it, but she had lost the world. She fell to the ground next to the child and cried. She cried until she forgot the word; then she reached out and touched the child. The child remained dead.

Slowly she rose, and she returned to Utopia. While all had watched her departure, no one, not even the gatekeeper, witnessed her return.

They were in council, deciding perfection.

In Eden, Utopia deflated and went flat, then flew off on the desert wind like a roll of thin parchment. Paradise rose up in its place, but she chased it away with her screams.

In the trees, the Serpent, coiled, awaited her.

In Eden, there were apples. Apples as large as elephant breasts. And the fruit flies sucked blood.

Adam, she cried out over and again, but the name came out "Mada-ada-da-manadam!" She tried to say the last two syllables by themselves, but it didn't work, so she screamed wordlessly and forced open her eyes and pressed against the ground. Her arms sank at first, like oars in water; then, in an instant, she stood. Before she could fall again, she ran.

She ran, even as the Serpent dropped from the trees and coiled about her and hissed its evil love into her ear. *Lick me,* it whispered. *Take me into your mouth, into your womb. Swallow me! Let me hide inside you.* . . . . Its tongue lashed her face, its tail pressed up between her legs. Its ecstasy made her reel. She forced her mind back to the child, the dead child in the forest, and she pushed the Serpent's tail away. But its whispers didn't cease, and its tail came back, thrusting into her.

Then she saw Stigg, like a rock growing out of the Earth.

Let it end! she screamed in her mind. *Let this end!* All this—Eden despoiled, and the other dream coming back to regain control. Attack it, she thought. *Make it absurd, make it unreal.*

She leaped at Stigg; anything was better than the Serpent. She crushed it between their bodies until it wimpered and crawled back into the trees. In her hand now, she held real sex—dream sex, but definitely male. With it, she would make it all go away—her negative selves, this false Eden, everything. *Reductio ad absurdum*—no dream could survive what she was about to do to this one.

She pushed him to the ground, then grabbed him again. The earth quaked as she slid down onto him and felt his fire inside her. Violently at first, then slowly, then violently again, she moved up and down until she came again and again and again, beating her hands and head against his chest until everything, at last, went black.

* * *

Stigg, still trembling, rolled Tiffany off of him, terrified, once again, that she was dying. But then, he realized, she kept acting like she was dying, but she never stayed that way.

He wished he'd found her sooner, before she'd found the danger place. Even so, as he rested on his side, looking down at her, he was glad Henna hadn't stayed with him. He wouldn't want Henna to see what had just happened.

As he picked Tiffany up, he remembered her screams and how they'd echoed through all his passageways below. He'd been sure she was dying then, but he'd thought the dark creatures had found her. She was so smooth. . . . Only after her screams had led him up, here, had he understood. But he still didn't understand the way she'd acted.

He felt bad now. He hadn't wanted to think of Tiffany like that. But she'd touched him. . . . It was the danger place. He knew it was the danger place.

It didn't matter now. He had to take her to Monk. With Tiffany tucked under one arm and his magic candle and map clutched in his other hand, Stigg headed back, underground.

XV.

Monk returned to the Batcave in early evening. To the best of his knowledge, he'd emptied the underground warren of his enemies of everything useful; what he'd left, he'd left for Algy. He had no desire to return to that place. Its polished walls and metallic surfaces stank of the sins and prides and deaths of the ancients. And nowhere—not in any of the crates—had he found guitars or drums or any of the other things he treasured, nothing to aid in dispelling the darkness in his heart.

Under other circumstances he might have retreated to transform the agonies of the previous night into eulogic ballads, something to heal the wounded souls of his people. But for that he would have needed time and understanding, and he had neither. Events demanded his presence, and the tidal furies roiling within him made understanding, as he knew it, as unattainable as the distant past that had reached out to bury its malicious claws in the hearts of Bobo, Bamph, Weezil, and Karmen. Karmen the blind—she came up to him as he entered, holding her hands before her, whispering his name, begging for his help. He held her, until Algy pulled her gently away and led Monk to the side to tell him of the day's events.

Algy related his observations of the morning and his subsequent meeting with Genie. Monk told Algy, as best he could, of the things they'd brought back from the underground home of the ancients. Their discussions were interrupted by the return of Henna, and the food carried by her and those with her managed, at last, to focus Monk's attention fully on the future. "Yes," he told Algy. "We may learn much from eating now. I'm glad you thought of it."

"I hadn't thought," Algy returned. "I don't think the soft food will have the effect on them. They are *ancients*. It is their food."

"I meant as much for us," Monk said. "For myself."

"You will eat?"

"If they will. We must make choices," he said solemnly. "And we'll remember them forever. If we decide wrong, it will be too late to undo. If we destroy them—as my heart pleads now that we should—we must be sure. I know that a pleading, on a day of deep sadnesses, is not an answer. We must have an *answer*."

"What if we find none?"

"We *must*," Monk said softly. "We must."

"They are both danger and knowledge." Algy glanced away, at the captives beyond the wire. "I learned that much today. They have wisdom, at least the one named Genie does. He said they might be able to make my flying machine fly."

Monk grunted. "Knowledge. All the knowledge we've ever sought, with death as its only price."

"We have taken their weapons. Normally, we play with their weapons."

"Not the ones that scorched the earth."

"I don't think these ancients have those weapons."

"Do you know that?" Monk asked. He stood silently for a while, his blue eyes gazing out at nothing; then he turned from Algy to address his people. "Tonight," he told them, "we feed the ancients the food of the ancients. I will eat as well. Any of you who also wish to eat may join us."

A few stepped forth from the crowd. Karmen stumbled again to Monk's side. "I will eat with you, my son," she said. "Perhaps I will find my eyes."

Monk looked at her, then glanced away, surprised at the speed at which tears had filled his eyes. "Perhaps," he told her.

Karmen, indeed, regained her vision. As Algy later related to Genie, her eyesight returned at the exact moment when Rachel, teary-eyed and totally oblivious to her own nudity, kissed Karmen on the forehead and whispered the last stanza of Coleridge's "Kubla Khan" into her ear. But Rachel did that to everybody that night, after she began to walk through the crowd like a glowing, primal incarnation of innocence and love.

For the feast, mats were laid out on the floor along the edge of the stage. The food—huge mushrooms, apples, peaches, and roots resembling yams—was spread all along the mats, interspersed with water and firewater held in containers of all shapes and sizes. Before Algy went to invite the ancients to join them, Monk, Karmen, and the few others who had decided to eat sat down, cross-legged, with their backs to the stage.

Algy went to Genie and told him all was ready and that Monk himself would dine with them. Several mutants made a parting in the wire, and Genie stepped through, followed by his men, Rachel, Jan, and Robert. Philip, Martin, and Madonna refused the invitation even though they were starving. Madonna would have eaten, but for her husband. Martin's parents, still seemingly in shock, showed no reaction at all to the development. Jan had begun to wonder whether they were, in reality, there. They had grown increasingly withdrawn; it was as if they hadn't fully wakened from the long sleep, and as if each hour carried them farther back into that eventless oblivion.

Jan, herself, could scarcely bear the noises of her own stomach; she didn't bother to argue with Philip when he refused—she simply rose to follow Genie, even though she knew she could easily persuade Philip and Martin to follow if she took the time for it. Their hunger was readily visible in their eyes; she would have paused and called back to them if she hadn't been thoroughly exhausted by their childish obstinacies already.

So she went to eat, wiping Philip and the tensions of the day from her mind like so many annoying cobwebs. By the time she sat, between Rachel and Genie, across from Monk, her brother seemed a world away.

Though at first he didn't intend to eat, Algy sat next to Monk to act as a bridge of language. Monk remarked that not all the ancients desired to eat, and Algy translated this.

"They're babies," Jan said, reaching for an apple, "and fools. They'll eat next time."

Monk smiled at her warily; then he, too, carried an apple to his lips. He began to tell them, through Algy, of his people's lore of the ancients. He spoke of the ancient towers he'd once discovered by crossing to the eastern island beyond which there was only water. Some of the towers—the buildings—still stood. There lived the masters of the ancients. They lived like ants in hills they built to the sky because that made their God happy. From there, with a happy God, they made all things; they made guitars and flying machines and picture stories and floating metal men and boom-balls. They also made the fires to kill themselves with, but before they did, they made the *greenplace* for the fathers of the new men, and they put food there for the new men to eat.

Then the fires came, and the *greenplace* almost didn't survive. But the next spring, the *greenplace* grew back, bigger than ever, and the fathers and mothers of the new men made their children that spring, and then they died. After that, only Monk was born. Monk was the newest man.

That was how they explained it, Algy said, translating for Monk and explaining also that, yes, they knew much more now about the ancients, but Monk was telling the old story.

Genie listened carefully and questioned Algy at the end. They were the very first generation after the nuclear devastation? They had lived thousands of years? As far as they knew—Algy replied—yes. Nobody actually remembered the fathers and mothers of the new men. What they did know was this: All of them—all but Monk—had grown from childhood together. They had lived together and survived together on their own. They were many thousands, maybe tens of thousands, more then, but most who had died had done so before the others had even learned their names. Or maybe they just didn't remember their names. Remembering that far back was difficult, even for Algy.

After the early years, though, death, except among the children they seemed fated never to have, had become rare. Before the previous night, the last deaths had occurred two centuries earlier—if Algy understood their counting of years correctly—when the beasts they named ophadragons, after monsters in one picture story, had come over the western mountains in hordes and tried to eat them. Three of Algy's people had died during the year it took them to kill half the ophadragons and chase the other half away.

By the time Algy had finished his explanation, Genie was no longer able to digest it all. At the first mention of ophadragons, Genie saw them: fierce, pink lizards with elephant trunks, shooting out of Algy's eyes and flying around over their heads inside the Batcave. A moment after that, he was alone in an African jungle, his body covered with ants, both inside and outside of his uniform. Though he could feel the insects, he ignored them; the hallucination had come on so quickly that he'd barely managed to recognize it as such. But he *had* recognized it—the ants were a real thing for him, for anyone like him who had lived and fought in jungles. They were a punishment for who and what he had been, but they couldn't possibly, actually, *exist*.

Had they been drugged? As a test? If so, he had to make sure they stayed calm. . . . He tried to speak, to warn his men, but no words came from his mouth. Desperately he reached forward, into the jungle. He felt a hand grip his, and Algy's head thrust suddenly through the foliage. "What . . . ?" Genie's voice unexpectedly came back. "Why did you do this to us? What did you give us?"

"Just the food," Algy said sincerely. "Are you in a

strange world? It shows us the strange world, too. I thought you would expect it, or I thought you would not see the strange worlds at all. This is the food of the ancients.''

''No, it isn't,'' Genie said, his voice a stream of color that pulled him, flying, into a night filled with stars and glowing, glittering birds that flew up, one by one, to whisper their names into his ear.

Jan first noticed something strange midway through Monk's story. She noticed that she heard it twice, once from Monk, then again from Algy. She understood Monk completely—so why was Algy echoing everything. Was he stupid?

No—he was transparent, she thought. Captured by ghosts, talking by ghosts talking echoes of ghostly echoes on her breasts and thighs and Philip you don't know what you're missing where's Tiffany?

What?

She was a swan, an eagle, a firefly. Hungry was the firefly, she ate.

Rachel never lost sight of the room; she fell in love with it after her first and only mushroom. It began simply enough—she rediscovered innocence, the gift that five-year-olds lose as they grow. It felt like flowers blooming within her—a field of daisies, dandelions, and marigolds under a blue sky dotted with tufts of cloud like unspun cotton, the down pillows of butterflies and swallows. Inside herself came a spring rain that washed everything filthy, everything tainted, from the soils of her field. Puddles ran into rivulets and streams, carrying away her aches and hurts, her fear and anger, leaving only a raw, smiling beauty that could speak equally to stars as well as men. To some extent, she knew the feeling because it was *in* her, an exuberant emotional reservoir she'd unwittingly tamed and focused into the vidlens. She'd ridden the waves of her gift to Hollywood during its darkest, wildest, most brilliant years, its twilight of glory when it looked out at the world, cried, and began to demand serious *Art* of itself. Even the Academy . . . too late, the Academy, but not too late for her. Her gift had carried her, comforted her, and protected her. Through her, it had shined its own light, dancing off her tongue at cocktail parties in small rooms where conversation banished dictatorships, abolished cruelty, and dropped acid in presidential brandy snifters. With glinting eyes that could make even the most jaded wax nostalgic over youth, she'd read Gurdjieff, Cocteau, and the lyrics of Kate Bush to all who would listen. And listen they had, captives chained as strongly as if she'd spoken words of her own making because they could sense them *inside* her, even if she couldn't. She'd understood it then as merely the passion of reading scripts, the translation of past poetry, timeless and transcendent. Now, after the mushroom, she learned the truth. She found her gift within herself, accepted it, and set about bestowing it upon others.

Monk became the first recipient of her love (a love without true object, because it manifested itself in everything upon which she gazed: Monk, Algy, her sister and brother, the food, the roof, her own hands . . .). During a moment when the others fell silent, Rachel fell forward and crawled over the mat, knocking over a flask of water with her hand, crushing peaches and the yamlike vegetables with her knees. She reached the ebon giant, reached out with a tender hand to touch his cheek, peered into his blue eyes, and said, "Love is like rainbows cast off a whirling prism. You have to catch the light, like—like . . ." It was then, grasping for words and gazing into the deep blue wells that were Monk's eyes, that the Coleridge lines seeped up through Rachel's memories. She said them to Monk, then she said them again, more loudly and emphatically, then softly, like a purring kitten. She fell onto her back and repeated them over and over again: *"And all who heard should see them there, and all should cry, Beware! Beware! His flashing eyes, his floating hair! Weave a circle round him thrice, and close your eyes with holy dread, for he on honeydew hath fed, and drunk the milk of Paradise!"* She rolled over food and drink, demanding the attention of all not carried away by their own visions. She grabbed a peach and bit into it, still repeating the lines; the juice of the fruit flowing out from the corners of her mouth as she arched her back, tossed the peach aside, and ripped open her blouse, rolling again until she'd struggled completely free of the cloth and shed, also, the jeans she wore. She came to rest, with another peach in her hand, in front of Algy. She kissed Algy's cheek, said to him the Coleridge lines, and pushed the peach into his mouth.

Without thinking, Algy took a bite. That was how he came to join in the feast.

After Algy, Rachel moved on, bestowing upon all she encountered a kiss and the short stanza of poetry, which grew more beautiful with each repetition as she discovered new ways to caress each word. To the mutants, these actions of an ancient seemed indescribably mysterious and wonderful. Her voice was like honey. The alien, lilting words and the fathomless compassion and love in Rachel's eyes made her more goddess than woman, and the simple fact of her existence, her *presence* among them, recalled without exception the *good* legends and tales, the old Earth, the kind Earth, the beautiful Earth, as if the fertile fields of innocence within her were tangible to all. By herself, without the benefits of a true comprehensible language, Rachel cured the wounded hearts of Monk's people and helped them to forget their dead, to make their dead seem unreal, or, more accurately, fated without a discernible, malevolent cause. Seeing Rachel and her innocent love, they could not believe that she—and, by extension, the ancients with her —were bad or evil.

And Rachel healed and helped others as well. When she reached Genie, the jungle horrors and ophadragons and whispering birds fled back into his subconscious, and after Rachel's departure, he was left at the side of a quiet pool, with Crystal, her long legs stretched luxuriously over the grass and her tongue beckoning him to draw closer. He did so, the palpable physical contact setting his senses on fire such that he could separate every aspect of her heady scent, feel every slight variation in her body heat, and see in her eyes every facet of her deep love for him. (In actuality, Genie was loving Karmen who, cured already by Rachel, had become much like her, a purring creature full of love and love for life.) Nothing drew Genie from this tranquil world until Algy, emerging from his own visions that he never divulged to anyone, grabbed Genie's hand and pulled him outside under the starlight, and then later to his lab where, as dawn cracked the horizon, Genie regained his tongue and talked away the morning hours, speaking for Algy of the past the old mutant so desperately desired to know.

Near dawn, Rachel made love with Monk. It wasn't a matter of preferential selection, neither was it truly a matter of lust. While Rachel had meandered lovingly through the group, naked and glowing like a goddess, she had miraculously done so without eliciting a sexual response. She hadn't had this effect consciously; indeed, had someone— anyone—touched her or attempted to take her, she would have willingly acquiesced and denied nothing. But those who had felt her love had felt something exceedingly subtle and fragile in its perfect tangibility, something that even thoughts of physicality might threaten to debase and make imperfect. No one tried to hold on to her, because everyone had felt that doing so might prove, tragically, that she was unreal. With Monk, it happened by accident, and it began when he laughingly tried to sing her words back to her. (This came after an equally hilarious attempt by Fiberglass Muskrat to take the stage, an attempt that resulted in nothing resembling a coherent, structured song.) Monk sang Coleridge back to Rachel, and when she turned to reply, she tripped and fell against his chest. Still laughing, Monk fell back with her, and they landed with her breasts pressed against his face. His muffled laughter brought to her lips what was, perhaps, her first deviation from the borrowed poetry during the entire night: Rachel said, "That tickles!" She slid down his body, but before she lifted her hips, she encountered Monk's reflexive physical response to their contact and, with that, her recitations of verse came to an abrupt end.

By this time, those of the mutants who had not joined at the feast's beginning had entered the hallucinogenic fray. To all, this union between the woman goddess of the ancients and their sole son, whom most revered as a god in his own right, sealed the bonds of love that Rachel had conjured from the jaws of tragedy and sorrow. The two became a centerpiece, an altar such that, for a while, all fell quiet, transfixed by the sight of Rachel's heaving breasts, Monk's hands as they traced lightly up and down her back, Rachel's deep red hair, and the sheen of sweat that covered the united bodies. Even Philip and Martin, who had tried to avoid watching the confused mass of bodies outside their cage, found themselves unable to ignore the gasps and moans that erupted out of the sudden silence. But though all watched and all listened, Rachel and Monk had discovered something inherently private, a joining of two unique visions that merged together with each caress. From the moment they'd touched, they'd lost awareness of everything but each other. To Rachel, the world was Monk's smooth, muscled chest; his kind, European face; his long, silky hair; and the endless blue of his eyes. To Monk, Rachel was an angel descended to banish his doubts, a sensual proof of the inherent decency of life, of man. She brought back for him the mystery that Tiffany had first instilled but that Bobo's death had dispelled.

So it went as the smooth motion of their joined bodies grew more rapid and Rachel's gasps and moans gave way to short, clipped shrieks. At the end, he pulled her down close to him, holding her close and forcing her to grind her hips against him in an attempt to prolong the final moments of ecstasy. During those moments, inside Monk, his internal war with Rachel's people, already gravely weakened by the previous events of the evening, ended like a song in mid-phrase, without a finale or even a resolving note, as if the tune itself were ill-fated, flawed from the start by some essential unreality that could not withstand the weight of physical scrutiny.

Here, from the union of Monk and Rachel, grew a true peace.

Jan and her brother Robert spent most of the night in private wonderlands of fabulous color and garbled words, and they began to emerge partially only during the surreal, timeless moments of Rachel's love. Still, neither moved until one of Genie's men, overcome by the sight of Monk and Rachel locked in a seemingly endless embrace of passion, lifted Jan from her place and laid her on the floor behind where she'd sat. Possessed by fragmentary after-images of Monk and Rachel that rapidly attained something of a mystical quality, as she had not *seen* her sister but had seen, rather, a faceless expression of transcendent love that created an emptiness inside her that yearned to be filled, Jan clutched at the man, thinking she'd been rescued by a Prince of the Seven Colors (who sang and danced and miraged like endless geese flunking into the horizon of absolute oranges . . .). After a time, her passions—and those of many others, for the love of Rachel and Monk infected the crowd like a plague—grew louder and wilder, and Jan came to attract and draw down to her anyone who came near, including, in the end, her brother—much to their later shame and the disgust of all family members who had not participated in the feast.

Late the following morning, after all who eventually slept had wakened, Monk decreed that a shelter be built outside the Batcave so that Rachel's people could live in the sun and the fresh air. Around the shelter they would place the wire, and the entrance would at all times be guarded: "Daughters and sons of the ancients," he called out. "This will be a prison only to those who choose it. Those who joined last night in eating the fruits of the *greenplace* are free to enter and exit at will, and they may live and sleep where they wish. Those who did not join may gain their freedom by offering to eat." His gaze fell heavily on Philip.

Algy busily translated. Philip shook his head defiantly at Monk. "Your whores are free, you mean," he said softly.

"Algy!" Genie shouted before the old one could translate Philip's words. "We cannot eat like that every day. We must have food—normal food."

"From where?"

"The crates," Genie offered. "Those crates you carried from our underground home. There will be food in some of them, food we can eat."

Algy told this to Monk, and the ebon giant looked at Genie and nodded. They spent the rest of morning, all of them, rummaging through the mound of supplies pillaged from the cryocomplex for vacuum-sealed and cryopreserved emergency rations that, to everyone's relief and to the credit of twenty-first-century technology, had not spoiled. The ancients took anything the mutants would allow them, clothes and any other items not military in nature.

Stigg's arrival with Tiffany punctuated the day's activities. The night before, he'd surfaced briefly, but he'd balked upon first entering the Batcave and realizing that those inside had eaten. He'd decided to wait.

Tiffany met her family there, at the mound of supplies. Tearfully reunited with Rachel and Jan (all too *real*), it all came together as she listened to Jan's explanation of the sequence of events and fitted that together with her own bizarre odyssey. The reality of what she'd thought a dream hit her with full, unforgiving force. Not much was said past that, for both Tiffany and Jan had deep, private guilts and fears to deal with on that day and for many days after that.

But on the whole, the three sisters, Robert, and Genie and his men were made as welcome as Monk and his people knew how. Genie and Rachel became confidants of the others, holding them together until each had aired his or her story in the open and felt, if not comfortable with it, then resigned to the reality of it all. And spirits rose two days later when Tiffany pointed out that the *profibervit* generator in the cryocomplex still worked, and Genie and Algy departed immediately on an expedition to bring a large supply of the tasty, nutritious cakes back for everyone.

During this time, Philip and Martin and the unfortunate Madonna stewed in self-inflicted frustration, refusing to have anything to do with their captors. They stayed, with Martin's parents, confined in the shelter. Jan's worries about Andrew Grant and Charlene Morrisey, that they'd somehow been revived from the long sleep too quickly, proved to be justified. After three days of captivity, having eaten nothing (when they were force-fed, they promptly vomited), the couple died, Charlene first, then Andrew, less than an hour after his wife.

Chapter

·5·

■ INSIDE A TEACUP, Daniel thought, may be clouds over a refined, Indian brew. Add a spoonful of sugar, watch the clouds, and he might learn the future.

Now, where had he heard that? Seen it? Experienced it?

It *could* have grown out of his mind, whole, never before formulated in another's thoughts. Or had his mind given birth to a variation on a theme—some civilized transposition of the reading of entrails, the interpretation of stars, the casting of sticks or bones? He might have draped an old thought in new fabric, and, at the same time, since he couldn't remember that particular image in any book he'd read or vid he'd seen, convinced himself that he'd made it up, however absurd or irrelevant it might be once applied to reality. But if it *was* an old thought, then this could be a universe in which only the thoughts were real, in which they flitted from mind to mind, over light-years and centuries, creating brief delusions of insight in the minds hosting them for insignificant slices of time.

A ghostly image of brains and streaking lights lingered behind his eyes like the afterburn of a long stare at the sun through the dark, polarized side of his sphere. The proposition reeked of absurdity, but he couldn't really *disprove* it. Within himself, underneath the mental language unique to his experience, he could sense a deep *affinity*, as if he were nothing but a receptor, for the ideas and feelings that his daily interactions with the vidscreen stuffed into his head, his vicarious understanding of a world that no longer existed, his proof of his own humanity. Throughout most of what he saw, he could easily draw parallel after parallel, essentially cornering everything into some vaguely understood distillation of all human expression. All stories, essentially, concerned life, movement, and time, all juxtaposed against some condition or conditions of existence. All thoughts came to him once formulated in a mind, a mind like his, a mind looking out, or a mind looking in. A mind in a specific place, location in space-time. Even what seemed the thoughts of his sphere—he knew they had once to be human. To all computers that applied; even machines designed by other machines couldn't think in ways that human logic couldn't verify.

So where did that leave original thought, and how could he question it? How could he *think* thought? What drove his mind from idea to idea like a hummingbird flitting from orchid to orchid, stealing nectar? Bad analogy? He'd never seen a hummingbird, not with his eyes, not independent of the screen through which he'd seen such wonders that a single hummingbird was but a small, insignificant speck of frantic life. And how did he know that? How did he know a hummingbird from a waterfall from a cloud from a 2031 Camairo? What size were all these things? Now, there was a question. . . . He knew the size of space; next to that, how could anything be large or small, how could anything be more than a speck? The Earth itself, home to thousands of Camairos, millions of waterfalls, and countless hummingbirds—even now it was scarcely larger than a bright star, and once, it had *been* but a speck, when his sphere had first pointed it out, there had been millions of stars brighter. And yet, he was to believe that all those things— waterfalls, Camairos, clouds, hummingbirds, and endless multitudes of other things—could be found there, or could once have been found there. How could he know all this, trapped in a space scarcely thirty feet across?

He lay on his bed, one year from Earthfall. He still had so much to write, and what he'd written already had added more to the others' confusion than dispelled it. He'd added to his confusion as well—some sequences had been so difficult, and others, Tiffany's dream sequences and the scene in Eden, had flown from him as if gifted with lives of their own, wings of their own, and he'd had but to give them the sky in which to fly. It had almost been like writing his own dreams; he'd found over time that, in his dreams, his life could be real. He could be Apollo, engaged in epic struggles across a tapestry of legend. He could be Gandalf astride Shadowfax; he'd even been Galadriel once. He'd climbed mountains next to the great monk Bodhihan. He'd piloted starships, and played chess with Einstein. In the Amazon basin, he'd charmed anacondas and made love to the wood nymph Alexis. All these things, he'd done, and they'd been real—he'd touched, tasted, felt things. From time to time, he'd wished he'd never wakened from the best of these dreams. At other times, he'd wondered where *they* came from, how his mind, when he slept, recalled the settings, the landscapes, the skies of Earth. All from the vidscreen, he knew. Every damned bit of it came from his small, transparent window into an extinct reality. He'd never seen such things with his eyes anywhere else, but, almost without exception, everything he saw on the screen was *fiction,* unreal by definition, staged. What did he know of real life, and how much of that knowledge still applied on an Earth bereft of civilization, of Hollywood and Sydney and Greensboro and Glasgow?

Only that of which Tiffany spoke could be real. Yet that world, the one he attempted to paint for the others, was more fantastic and less believable than nearly anything on the vid. As Daniel thought about it, he himself was fantastic. He and his sisters and cousins, floating slowly through space back to Earth, were equally unbelievable. In relation to most of the vid, his own story would be science fiction, like *Star Wars* or *Foundation* or *Spring Break on Ganymede.* Only he didn't feel like an actor. He felt terribly alone, and desperate to taste the air of a real, unmanufactured atmosphere.

He supposed the worst part was his mother. He could never see her again, even if she still lived. She could never be more than a memory, a voice from the cube, a teacher, an adviser, but never a mother, not in the way he knew of motherhood from the vid. It felt strange; one of Diane's recent requests for his writing was "More sex!" As if she hadn't been able to realize that what he wrote was supposed to have *happened,* that he wrote about their parents, that they were supposed to feel some connection, some invisible but inbreakable umbilical cord, and that was supposed to make them feel something *more.* But to Diane, himself, and surely Monica and David as well, their mothers remained forever young, heroines of a book, unreal, never really mothers. And the sex excited Diana, not just the sex in Tiffany's story, but the sex in the vid as well. It excited Daniel when he thought about it, and he knew his sister and David were no exceptions; they were all discovering sex, alone in their spheres, and they all knew that puberty was irreversible. These realizations brought with them all the excitement, curiosity, nervousness, and worry that they'd brought to every adolescent in human history. But in their case, at the end of history, Daniel sensed irrevocable tragedy; he'd had more questions about Jan's guilt over making love with her brother than about anything else. They'd all heard of incest, but until Daniel had censured it, established it by Jan's guilt, they'd never felt that the taboo applied to them. All the questions came, therefore, out of guilt for loving one another, desiring one another after suddenly learning that, even in their family, it was still wrong. But they had no certainty of human life beyond themselves. Even if they reached Earth, who else might they find to love?

For all of Tiffany's wisdom and care, she hadn't anticipated this. Daniel wondered whether she'd missed the possibility because it had dwelled outside the realm of tasteful contemplation, because it was a thought that mothers couldn't easily think about their own children, no matter what the circumstances. Tiffany had understood deeply, though, the basic lack of family ties they would experience. "Keep us young in your hearts, Daniel," she asked him, with a choked voice as if she held back tears. "We gave life to you, but we can never be mothers. Mothers raise children, and we can't do that for you. So you should see us as people, people who love you, but still people, real and imperfect, and subject to all the failures of the human heart. That is why I'm telling you these things, my dreams and my nightmares. You need to know what our lives were really like. As I talk to you—for me, some future you—I find I can hold back nothing. Mothers lie to their children to protect them; I can no longer protect you, so I cannot lie."

And Daniel knew that Tiffany was right. They had never been a *family;* they could never even *be* one, not mothers and children, but also not sisters and brothers and cousins the way they were supposed to be.

They'd each spent too many years absolutely and utterly alone for that, nearly nine years before the first words had begun to pass between them, and since then they hadn't been able to touch like family; they'd only been able to yearn. And yearning was unreal, unable to substantiate the relationship and make it whole, especially when, to each other, they were the sum known total of humanity.

So he wrote for his human race, his audience of three, four if he counted himself, eight if he counted the spheres and assumed they actually understood something of what got read to them. Sometimes Daniel wondered if the spheres didn't understand more than David—his cousin was cracking; he'd come to think of his sphere as truly human, and he wrote poems to it:

Keep me in your womb,
Where the sun can't burn me, where you read to
  me,
Where you love me at night, feed me in the morning,
And rain tears for me when I cry.

It sounded to Daniel as if he hadn't been the only one to have problems with atmosphere regulation systems. But it was worse than that. Sometimes several days would pass when none of them, not even Diane, would get a single word from David. And whenever David started to write, poems would come more often than not. Then silence again. Daniel tried to imagine David's days of silent retreat from their impossibly small community, what went on his mind, what vid he watched, what music he listened to. But beyond that, even Daniel dared not go—he *couldn't* make himself think himself into David's world of impending, certain death in solitude. They all knew that, short of a miracle, David was going to die, alone in space.

Daniel couldn't think of that for himself; only by thinking of life, only with hope, could he go on. And only with his writing. It felt like his now—Tiffany's world. So much like his that he wanted to change it, make it more happy, spend days writing of the good times, of the wordless love that Rachel and Monk shared, of the long, gin-soaked conversations under the moonlight when Tiffany and Jan managed to find peace enough to talk, when Genie ("like a fatherly teddy bear," Tiffany said) told his own story and related his own thoughts in loving detail and encouraged everyone to do the same. But those conversations, those nights, were the source of much of the story, and not the story itself.

Yes—the story itself. Sometimes days would pass when he'd write scarcely more than a few sentences and spend the rest of his time in creative anguish, seeking an approach and trying, still often in vain, to understand it all himself. The food—he had no way to experience it himself. ("Your dreams, Daniel," Tiffany said, "hear my words and think of your dreams." But he was *already* writing a lot about dreams! What was the difference?) He knew something about gin; the sphere could make it for him if he asked, but he didn't really like the taste. He enjoyed it only after he'd drank so much that the taste didn't make a difference, and then he always fell asleep too quickly to get much out of the experience. The food, though—when he tried to describe it for his sphere, the sphere never understood.

Then the questions kept coming from the others, many about the things that Daniel himself didn't understand, so how could he hope to answer? Those aside, Monica kept jokingly goading him about the natures of the mutants, how he had to be making them up, how they couldn't possibly be explained by a simple nuclear war, especially after he'd implied that they hadn't evolved, but had all been living since shortly after the end of the world Tiffany had known in her youth. Questions like that, Daniel refused to answer out of context. He did, however, admit to them that he knew nothing more about Benson the Barstool. The amorphous creature never appeared after Tiffany's first night out of the cryocomplex; for all Tiffany knew, it lived in the Batcave, and it lived only to be sat on. For reasons known only to itself, it had stayed out of the way during that time when the ancients had been caged within the walls of its home. Daniel actually wondered on one occasion whether Tiffany had made Benson up, whether in her memory she'd mixed up a real dream or two with the perceived dream. But if he believed that, maybe nothing was real. . . . Maybe they were all still parts of Tiffany's dreams. What would happen if she ever woke up? Curious, he thought; he'd read theories of God that sounded a lot like that.

Some of the other questions he received were funny, while others would hurt: At the same time Diane had requested more sex, she'd asked why he didn't write more about Robert, their mother's good brother. How could he tell her, flatly, that Robert died? How could he explain briefly how that death had come too soon, and how it had ended a quiet life that hadn't *needed* to open up with its experiences because it hadn't really been hurt by them? Robert wasn't smart; in fact, he was quite stupid and wise enough to remain generally silent because of it, but he'd *cared*. That care had killed him.

Daniel knew, as he reflected on these things, that what remained for him to write would be the hardest of all. So far, only he could truly guess what might await them on Earth. So far, he'd kept secrets, and, with parts of the story, he'd made his sister and cousins happy. Monica had never stopped sending him pictures: He had almost fifty pictures of Monk alone, and, when he thought about it, he realized that Monica had illustrated more of Tiffany's story than he himself had told. Diane kept up with it all, but nothing worried her more than her studies and David. David wrote his poems and would emerge with lucid thoughts from time to time. . . . Perhaps, Daniel thought, he should hurry to the story's end if only to let David know how uncertain and lonely all their futures might be. Nothing—not even Earth—was certain.

But Daniel couldn't let himself believe that. Not yet.

"Everything happened so quickly, Daniel. . . ."

What if it hadn't? What if people had taken time to stop and think?

"It all began," Tiffany said, *"with Robert's death."*

·EARTH·

PART THREE

I.

Robert Tyler-Grant died as meaninglessly and unnecessarily as had his aunt and uncle before him. He died instantly, in the late-night darkness of early morning, one month after Tiffany's fateful escape from the long sleep.

Robert's death wasn't an accident; he was murdered.

Along the south side of the mutant community, three squat, brick buildings sprang up from the earth like dilapidated, stunted progeny of the Batcave in the north. In their shelter, most of Genie's men sought refuge from the midday sun, and they returned there at night to sleep. Half the time, Robert stayed with them. Of all the Grant family, even under circumstances adverse enough to shatter the most rigid of societal barriers, only Robert went to any real lengths to extend friendship to the relatively uneducated, raucous group of young mercenaries who had been lured into the Grants' folly of survival with payments of gold and promises of a brave new world. Robert extended his friendship because he had nothing else to do: He was too simple to attempt meaningful communication with most of the mutants, his sisters had too many other things on their minds, and his brother and cousin looked upon him as a fool and a traitor. With the young men, he could relax, tell and hear jokes, sing, and drink. Genie—so wrapped up in his philosophizing, his fascination with Algy, and his concern for Robert's sisters—paid little attention to his men once the tensions between the ancients and the mutants had relaxed. After all, he knew that they knew they'd been defeated, and he knew that, like young men in the old days, they'd make the best of their idle time, filling it with parties and music, especially music after Fiberglass Muskrat resumed its nightly festivals of electric noise. Besides, the simpler mutants—many of them quite exotically attractive—welcomed the infusion of new faces with uninhibited pleasure. Genie never interrupted the continuous party except to borrow particular talents that he himself did not possess.

Robert threw himself into the middle of it all, and, in the process, made friends with Stigg. Each of them seemed to find comfort in the other's silly smile. Once the bond between them had formed (and the method of this bonding forever remained a mystery to Tiffany), Robert and Stigg seldom did anything alone, a development all the more astonishing because they didn't share a common tongue but managed in spite of it to forge a bizarre linguistic bridge that nobody on either side of the cultural barrier ever professed to understand. Yet it happened, and for a time the pair were perhaps the most happy of all. For the last two weeks of Robert's life, Stigg forsook his underground home, and, for the first time in anyone's recent memory, he lived among the others.

Tiffany, though it made her feel guilty, encouraged the relationship, if only to deflect Stigg's attention from herself. Robert was like her little brother who had never grown. He'd been the family's greatest failure, and he'd spent seven years in high school before they'd given up on his abilities and bought him a diploma. Since then, he'd been their resident idiot; Tiffany suspected that this alone might have explained his empathy toward Stigg. They shared the bliss of ignorance between them, and, as for Stigg, whose devotion to her never waned, she felt he might have adopted Robert as a surrogate for herself; she'd had the specifics of her physical similarities to her brother drilled into her head since childhood. They had the same brown eyes; the same slender, slightly hooked nose; and the same flat, square chin, but so did most of the rest of their family.

The afternoon before Robert died was particularly hot, the sort of heat that induced sleep, rolling across the desert like the opium-laden breath of the dragons of dream. Those refusing to succumb were beaten down, numbed by the relentless sun, which corrupted even the coolest of shades. In days past, Tiffany had never known such heat; she'd lived an air-conditioned youth of swimming pools and ice cream parlors. Never this kind of heat, except in a sauna.

By this time, Tiffany shared a small, comfortable building with her sisters. She'd spent the morning talking with Jan, drinking water and wishing for the coffee she knew she'd never taste again. A few days before, Tiffany had finally confessed to Jan some of the finer, more obscure details of her story, and one detail had caused them, more and more often, to seek out privacy for their talks. It was the detail of her father, his intrusion into what she'd thought a dream, when she'd sat at one of Medusa's remote consoles and suffered her father's nagging demands until she'd overridden his authority. Now Tiffany realized she hadn't dreamed, and that meant something ominous: Her father—their father, and hence in all likelihood, Mother Grant herself—knew something of what had transpired.

"They'll write us off," Jan would keep saying under her breath, and Tiffany could only nod, weakly attempting to forge a consensus, though neither of them truly believed it. It didn't fit with the ways of the *family*. "That's why she put us by ourselves," Jan would insist. "She planned from the beginning to use us as bait, to test the future. She never liked any of us much except Philip, and I was never honestly sure she liked him. But her real favorites, Mason and Jonathan, and our wonderful dad and that little worm she grew in a test tube—she kept all of them with her. She must have watched what happened to us and decided to throw us away. I'll bet Dad's asleep already, waiting for another few thousand years to pass. She probably set up her complex so they could sleep indefinitely."

It still didn't sound like the family.

Tiffany wanted to believe her. The mere possibility of truth in Jan's hypothesis kept them from discussing it with anybody else. Even Rachel—so far, nobody had told the mutants that more ancients still slept underground somewhere nearby. They knew that if Monk knew, everything might change again. Had Monk known English, Rachel probably would have told him anyway; thankfully, neither Monk nor Rachel felt a deep need for verbal communication in their relationship. But if Rachel knew what Tiffany did —that recent events had alerted and wakened at least one of the human sleepers in Complex One—Tiffany and Jan felt their sister's heart might easily overpower her sensibilities. For the same reason, they'd elected not to tell Genie. The old soldier almost looked young again, and he talked of their predicament as if they'd found a fantasy world, and he'd already expressed to them his growing belief that the rest of the Grant clan had elected to forget them. "All the better," he would say. "We don't need them, do we?"

For Genie and his men, and for Robert and Rachel, maybe that was true; war no longer hung over their heads, and they had no reason to work or to fight for survival. But the fantasy, for both Tiffany and Jan, had been indelibly tainted. Events had condemned them to a limbo between a past of madness and a future of unforgiving guilt, Jan for what she'd done blindly in hallucinogenic lust, and Tiffany for the same, made worse because she pitied Stigg, and even worse because that pity could almost make her believe she desired him again.

Tiffany had other troubling guilts as well. She knew, deep within herself, that all this *was* her fault. She'd treated reality as a nightmare, and treated it frivolously, irresponsibly. If she'd taken charge that first night, somehow handled herself and the situation at the scene of Bobo's death, she might have been able to stop Genie's charge. Men had died that night—men she'd seen but never known, and now their faces came to her at night, a procession of broken dreams and wasted lives. Many times since rejoining her family, she'd relived her first vision in Eden, that of the wounded, limping soldiers, but death didn't just haunt their gazes, it lived there, and she'd shown it the way. She'd inflicted the wounds; she'd sated Death's hunger after its centuries of starvation. If she'd had herself together that first night, if she hadn't been thinking of how wonderful it was to be free and thought more instead on how she'd happened to be free, maybe no one would have needed to die. Maybe even Bobo could have lived; she knew now that Philip had killed him.

She often thought of Bobo, of his limp form and the horrible wound in his eye (he was the Oedipus in her first vision in Eden, the counterpoint of the wounded soldiers, the casual link that had made the vision complete and given it retrospective sense). Every time she saw Fender Fang, who had left for a period of solitary mourning shortly after the night of the battle, Tiffany thought of Bobo, the first casualty. The huge dog sent her spirits plummeting. For two weeks, she would have sworn the dog itself was a ghost for the way it lumbered sadly through the town, heedless of mutant and ancient alike, sniffing along the streets as if in search of its master. She grew convinced that it still lived only after Philip, foolishly, howled maniacally at it from his wire cage. Fender had come alive then; if Monk hadn't been near to stop the dog, Tiffany was sure it would have bitten Philip in half.

All this weighed heavily on Tiffany's heart, and when the sun on the afternoon before Robert's death began to pound at it, it made it more heavy, drilling it deeper, spreading it over her mood like dark pastels over a reluctant but defenseless canvas.

She would have slept, as Jan went to do and as Rachel had all morning, but Jan reminded her that it was her turn to carry the buckets of water to Philip, Martin, and Madonna.

Walking was like swimming, the hard ground like a boiling mud that wanted to suck her down into a burning embrace. The heat—it had never been like this before; Tiffany blamed it dully on the lack of trees—nothing to suck the carbon dioxide out of the atmosphere anymore. The greenhouse effect of the twenty-first century had been bad enough . . . but this? Christ, it had to be a hundred in the shade! And, according to Philip, it was supposed to be springtime still. What on earth would summer be like?

She moved slowly, silently, and made no attempt to speak to Fredo, who sat, head bowed, on the ground next to the cage, derelict in his duty of guarding her brother. And that is how she came to hear him.

The words at first seemed a delusion of the heat. The pieces she understood seethed and whispered, like the snake in Eden: *". . . but I don't know where . . . the big black one, yes . . . definitely."* If Tiffany had been thinking clearly, she might have paused and listened longer. As it was, she burst in on Philip, and she didn't really understand what she'd heard until she saw him, communipact in hand, his eyes rising to meet hers, his hand—too slowly—moving to conceal the device.

He'd had it all this time; he'd salvaged it from the pile of supplies that Monk had recovered from the cryocomplex. For the gullible mutant watching him, he'd pretended to eat it.

"What are you staring at?" he asked Tiffany nervously, hoping that he'd hidden the communipact in time but already realizing, by the dull astonishment in Tiffany's eyes, that he'd failed.

Tiffany dropped the buckets of water; one of them spilled over, splashing its contents onto Martin and Madonna, who had been curled together, asleep, against the wall of the shelter.

Martin bolted awake, glaring at Tiffany. "You stupid bitch! You can't—"

"Shut up, Martin!" Philip seethed desperately, never taking his eyes off his sister. "It's not what you think, Tiff!"

For long, tense moments, she fought to find her voice. The communipact—the small, everyday artifact of her past—made plain everything she didn't want to believe: Somewhere, with Philip as an accomplice, the rest of the family plotted. "What," she replied numbly, "that you're going to get us all killed?"

He stared back wordlessly.

"Who was it, Philip? Father? Mother Grant?"

"Mother Grant," he said without expression.

"Are they all awake now?"

"I guess so. I don't know."

"Wonderful."

"You can help us now, Tiffany," he pleaded. "We've got to get out of this!"

"And into what? Death? Don't you know when you're beaten?"

"Look who's talking!" Martin spat viciously. "You're the one who got us into this! You and your whore sisters!"

"Enough, Martin!" Philip said, unable to maintain his whisper. "They're blood. Family!"

"They're whores. Let 'em die humping those monsters."

Tiffany didn't stay. She picked up the second bucket of water, threw it on Martin, and left without another word.

II.

In late afternoon, Tiffany and Jan found themselves restless, reluctant participants in the daily drinking bout they'd come to call the sunset gathering. Rachel, who'd risen in the wake of the midday heat, dragged them there, thinking their obvious sleeplessness a sign of renewed depression and future shock that needed only a little group therapy and sufficient alcohol to cure. In actuality, Tiffany had wakened Jan immediately upon her return from Philip, and they'd spent their time since then trying, unsuccessfully, to persuade themselves out of the despair Tiffany's discovery had crystallized with alarming certainty:

No longer could they hope for or assume abandonment by their grandmother. Their every thought of the future now had to take into account the rest of their family. And no matter how tragic the outcomes they could picture, their own unspoken discomfort with the lives thrust upon them made any perspective wholly involving staying with the mutants difficult. They had no certain loyalties, and no certain desires except a desire for the world they'd known but lost, for its people, its mysteries, its sense of adventure, its sense of infinite *un*certainty. Here they had a world of menacing horizons, complicated by now by the fact that their bodies had not yet resumed menstruation, and they didn't know whether this was a side effect of the long sleep, or whether it meant what they feared so deeply that they never mentioned: pregnancy. Rachel had voiced the concern over her own body's failure to function, but none of them had dared to ask Madonna, especially as she remained forever in the presence of her unbearable husband.

On the other side—Philip's side—was a nightmare of subservience to family. Maybe Mother Grant would still do nothing, or maybe she waited for a simple way to "rescue" them from their captors. Maybe—it still didn't sound like family. Everything they understood about their grandmother made them fearful that she might look upon the invincible mutants as a challenge, the ultimate test of her self-importance and superiority. She might decide to conquer for the simple fact that the mutants were there; for the same reason, she'd led her family underground to await the future, because the future was there, and because she'd bled the present until the present was dry. And once she'd made the decision, she'd ordered it, leaving no room for argument, implying threats of death when all other persuasions failed (Tiffany hadn't heard these, but Jan had. Jan had hated the idea of abandoning her life, however tenuous her future might have been.)

But maybe Mother Grant would act wisely. Maybe the rest of the family, when and if it emerged, would make things better, not worse. Maybe their fears were unfounded, and their grandmother had grown benevolent during her years of dreaming.

Maybe.

An exhausted grin spread across Genie's face. "Well," he said, "the flyer should work now. We've checked it over and over again for the past three days; Algy did an incredible job of getting it all together right in the first place."

"Luck," Algy said, but he couldn't suppress his own broad smile.

"Come on, ladies!" Genie said. "At least look excited! We only need fuel and oil now."

"Not so easy," Jan interjected blandly. "You try to put anything but the right nitromix in that thing, and you're likely to blow yourselves up."

Genie shrugged her off. "Give us some credit! Maybe we'll find old tanks. . . . Come on, think! With the flyer airborne, the whole planet can be ours. Beyond the mountains and oceans, we might find other life, other pockets of survival, maybe even other technologies, enough to get us to the other side of the world. We can build a civilization again, but do it right this time! Communication, brotherhood. . . ."

He went on: They could construct a global language; resurrect the arts; excavate the past; collect, understand, and reevaluate human history and knowledge. . . .

Maybe, Tiffany thought darkly. Somewhere nearby, Genie probably could find several other flyers, fully fueled, probably battle-equipped NP tri-jets. Not in the sky—not yet. But her grandmother had them as certainly as she had every other damned thing she'd felt she might need for her foray into the future. That list had to include flyers. They hadn't had them at Complex Two, but that had been a mere outpost. Tiffany, like all those with her, knew nothing of the main complex (evidence in itself of Mother Grant's paranoid, megalomaniacal foresight), so she could only guess at its secrets and wonder and fear at how and when they might materialize.

Monk, hearing Genie's words through Algy's softly spoken translation, kept an arm around Rachel and an unfathomable, vaguely ironic smile on his lips. Perhaps he sensed in Genie's enthusiasm an innocence or a desperation of spirit that betrayed the very aspects of the old humanity's downfall, its insatiable thirst for knowledge coupled with an inherent desire for control, its wealth of visions, beautiful until the inevitable clashes when they transformed unexpectedly into dark parodies of themselves in their attempts to overcome and attain that ever-elusive control, like the Russias and Americas Algy had explained to him countless times over. Perhaps Monk thought these things, or perhaps he thought of other things: Rachel under his arm, the music he would play later that night, or the songs he was writing. Perhaps his smile meant only that he had his life and his happiness and he didn't really care what happened with the flyer as long as it made Algy and Genie happy, which it obviously did. He didn't, during the conversation, offer words one way or the other.

So the evening passed with Genie animate, Rachel occasionally placing a hand on one of her sisters' in well-intentioned concern, and Tiffany and Jan doing their best not to let their eyes stray to nervously scan the horizon.

That night Fiberglass Muskrat played, and the youngest of the Tyler-Grant sisters refused to let her elders out of her sight. She insisted they join her at the front table to watch and listen to her lover. The ritual, and it had become virtually a nightly one, grated on Tiffany in her present state of mind. But she didn't know how to refuse it gracefully, and the music from time to time, in its unique, overpowering way, did manage to relegate her worries to the back of her mind temporarily.

As it was, nobody noticed exactly when Stigg and Robert disappeared to take a long walk in the moonlight. Nobody even suspected anything might have happened until the next day, when Robert wasn't to be found anywhere and when Stigg's underground home, upon inspection, proved uninhabited. They had no answer until late that evening when Fender Fang led them to a low mound of packed earth under which they found Robert, the shaft of a hypodart deep inside in his chest.

Tiffany, staring unbelievingly down at her dead brother, realized then how expendable they all were. She didn't learn until later that Robert had died foolishly in a futile attempt to save his friend from a battle droid's tranquilizer hypodarts. After Robert's fall, Stigg had stood still, and the next dart had found his eye.

Now both sides had captives.

"Your father, Daniel—he was as innocent as they come. But he cared. You know, one day he came to me with this rock in his hand. I guess it was about three times the size of my fist, but it fit easily in his palm.

"I was hot and sweaty, digging through our stack of supplies, looking for something that didn't taste like chicken. God, I must have looked a mess, dirt streaked all over my face, and I could barely stand the smell of myself. Stigg just planted himself in front of me. 'Pretty Tiffany,' he said—of all things, 'Pretty Tiffany' like when we first met. I looked like hell. He said 'Pretty Tiffany' and started rubbing this damned rock under his armpits. I looked at him and he grinned, then he tried to hand me the rock.

"I tried to ignore him, but he wouldn't leave. I didn't know what the hell he was trying to do. Finally we got into

one of those strange sign-language bouts—always confusing. All I could figure was that he wanted to take me somewhere. He'd rub that rock under his armpit, then make some walking signs with his fingers. . . .

"He took me to a pool where I could take a quiet bath, you know? How did he know that's what I'd dreamed of all morning? Robert probably put him up to it. . . . Usually, every other evening or so, we'd all troop off together to bathe in a river about a quarter-mile away. But everyone went at the same time, and it was never relaxing, especially when us girls knew that, just around the bend, was a horde of horny, naked men—uh, if you don't understand what I mean, Daniel, don't worry about it.

"Anyway—this pool! Cool, shaded water! Crystal clear . . . as clear as the sky. I looked at it like a dream come true. Tried to get Stigg to leave me there, but he wouldn't go. Finally I just stripped and hopped in. Wasn't as if he hadn't seen me that way before.

"He just sat there at the pool's edge, rubbing that stupid rock under his armpit and grinning like he'd done the most incredible thing imaginable. Maybe that bit with the rock was his idea of bathing—I don't know; maybe it was his idea of my idea of bathing. . . . I almost wish now I'd invited him in.

"Anyway, I must have stayed in the pool for hours. . . ."

III.

Her real name was Madeline Delarue before she'd married Robert Travis Grant, Jr., son of the founder of Grant Technology and Enterprise who had forced his company through bribes and government contracts to the cutting edge of technological research by the turn of the twenty-first century.

Grant had gotten its fingers in the government pie in just about every area of research imaginable, from basic physics and chemistry to aerospace design, genetic engineering, communications, and pharmaceuticals, the last being its gold mine, its guarantee forever of financial security once the royalties for its alcohol counteractive, "Buzz Buster," began rolling in. (That product had catered to a built-in, high-priced, market; America's courts, by then, took a very dim view of drunk drivers, and the wealthy, of course, would pay anything to avoid a hangover.)

To the outside, Grant T & E seemed remarkably blessed; few realized that corruption and industrial espionage had been its strong suits from the beginning. Madeline Delarue had been one of the few; she'd known because her father, also a ruthless man but a competitor of the Grants, had told her.

She'd known other secrets that only the wicked of the world could share: Robert Grant, Sr., a proud man with a warped but strong sense of honor, lost his young, beautiful wife, Angelique Simone, in 1994 in a battle of the industrial war—not in a simple automobile crash, as the media had reported. Madeline had known this because her father had ordered Angelique's death out of spite after losing a critical contract to Grant T & E. *Very* few people knew any of this, but the facts did eventually filter down through the later Grant generations as half-whispered legend, mainly because Madeline didn't care. She was proud of her past.

By 2012, the Delarue family, paupered and embittered, sent Madeline, deadly beautiful and all of seventeen, to exact their final revenge on the Grants. Robert Grant, Sr., had never married after Angelique's death, and Madeline was to infiltrate his defenses, seduce him, and murder him in his sleep. She got as far as getting him alone in his room, at which point he'd turned to her and said, "I know who you are, and why you're here, and I only let you get this far because I like you. If you want into this family, say so. If you don't, then leave.''

Madeline said yes, and later that night, Grant operatives murdered her father in *his* sleep. She never looked back. Though she did seduce Robert Grant, Sr., he refused to marry her himself, but two months later she found herself at the alter next to his son. From that point on, year by year, the reins of Grant T & E came into her hands, so that by the time the founder officially retired in 2035, Madeline Grant was the undisputed monarch of the company and one of the wealthiest, most powerful women in the world. She'd carried the company through Moral Prohibition, privatizing ownership and shedding, during that time, all but the most minor government contracts and emerging, somehow, stronger than ever. The Republican Party, in its death throes before its merger with the Democrats, all but begged her to run for president, and VidScoop and other media were forever comparing her to Britain's legendary Iron Lady, Margaret Thatcher.

She didn't run for president, of course. She remained quite content to run her own private empire. She did what she wished; when she wanted something, she'd buy the company that made it if that's what it took. She even stole a spaceship from SubSpace Corporation the year after Magnus disappeared and the rest of mankind had thought his technology lost forever.

As for the family, there were no living Grants, except her husband and the ancient Thelonius, her husband's uncle, who did not have some of her blood in their veins. All of them, though, without exception, called her Mother.

The youngest of her four sons, named after her husband and his father, was only fifteen and hence the youngest member of the family when they'd gone underground to leave the twenty-first century behind. Like Andrew, her third son, the third Robert Travis Grant had never known the inside of her womb; Madeline's biotechs had grown him in an artificial womb after successfully fertilizing one of her preserved eggs with her husband's preserved sperm. Thus did she herself bring new life into the family after all her grandchildren had grown.

The third Robert Travis Grant was the human responsible for his nephew Robert's death.

On the night Robert murdered Robert, Madeline Grant sat behind her son and watched him gleefully work the controls of the battle droid. A remote sensor, planted earlier in the week, had notified them of the presence of two moving bodies while Mother Grant had been sipping sherry and telling her youngest son of her youth while the others slept. When Medusa informed them of the development, they decided to handle it alone. They'd waited long enough as it was; Philip no longer had anything new and useful to tell them.

So Robert Travis Grant worked the droid. On the part of Mother Grant, allowing the boy this was not unwise: He *was* the most talented human operator at her disposal, having mastered the machine almost as soon as he'd grown big enough to reach all the controls. She watched him, still sipping her sherry. Neither of them could have helped young Robert's death, really. He just jumped in the way of a hypodart far too powerful for a normal human.

"I killed him," Robert Travis Grant said finally, after examining the fallen bodies.

"The mutant?" the old woman asked.

"No. I killed Robert."

"Well, never you mind," she said. "Bury the little moron, and nobody will know the difference. But hit the mutant again, so he doesn't wake up."

"Yes, Mother," he said, drilling another hypodart into

the mutant's eye after dislodging the first to allow a deeper penetration into the same wound.

"Good boy. Medusa!"

"Yes, Mother Grant."

"Alert the biolab and security. Tell 'em we finally got one."

IV.

Before Fender Fang arrived to lead the way to Robert's body, Algy and Genie decided to investigate a hunch—a wrong hunch, but it gave Genie the final piece of a puzzle.

They knew that Stigg had found Tiffany in the *greenplace*. Excepting Stigg's tunnels, that was the only place Algy could imagine Stigg getting lost. Besides, Genie had asked several times to see it, and now they had a perfect opportunity to forget Algy's lab for a while and explore. Nobody yet thought that anything terrible had happened.

"Don't eat," Algy reminded him as they neared it. "Don't drink, and you might try not touching anything. Your skin is quite uncommonly thin."

"I'm okay," Genie said, tapping his shoulder to remind Algy of his pack. "As long as it's okay to breathe."

Algy smiled. "It should be."

Among the trees and springs, Genie found his last memory of Crystal resurfacing. Almost exactly like this, he thought. The pool, the trees, the sun . . . if he squinted, he could almost see her there on the grass.

The *greenplace* was a gently sloping hill; the very life of the place hit Genie full force, so long had he been starved of such sights. A month before—a forever before—he had been in such a place. The pool . . . hadn't there also been a hill? Could this be the very place he'd given Crystal her perfect day? He was half tempted to walk around the perimeter of the hill, looking for the exact pool, the exact trees. But no, four millennia had made pointless that approach. Some trees, he knew, could live that long, but not these oaks and elms and fruit trees, renegades from some long-forgotten orchard. How had this place survived while the rest of the land went barren?

They climbed slowly to the hilltop and wandered.

"You say you were born here?" Genie asked.

"Yes. All of us."

"I guess I can believe that."

"You have to. It's true. This place enslaved us. It gave us names for everything in it."

Genie laughed. "What's the name of that tree, then?" he asked, pointing at an oak.

"I don't know," Algy said. "It's new."

"Had to be some like it way back when."

"Some like it, yes," Algy countered, "but not that one."

"You had individual names for everything?"

"Yes." Algy laughed. "That pool there—he's called Aeroo. He's old, but I still recognize him. He wants us to drink from him, but we won't."

Genie frowned at him.

"Don't disbelieve me." Algy chuckled. "I'm serious. This is a powerful place. You should know—you ate the food. We *lived* here. We lived here and ate and drank every day. Had you found us then, you would have thought us mad, like animals."

"Monk led you away?"

"Yes. When he grew up, he told us we could go away and forget the names. He went out into the yellow lands and learned there were other things we could eat."

"How did he know?"

"I don't know. I've never asked."

"Maybe Aeroo told him."

"Maybe."

They wandered, and Genie found the past instead of Stigg and Robert. It jutted out of a gully in the form of a weathered granite slab, a piece of wall.

"There's a building under here!"

Algy drew up next to him. "Feela," he said.

"What?"

"Feela. That's Feela—her name."

"It's a building!"

"Probably—there are many buried buildings. Everywhere there are buried buildings."

"But this one's *here*! Do you know what it was? Is there a way inside?"

"There are tunnels," Algy said. "We could get lost—did you bring a lantern?"

Yes, Genie had—in case Stigg and Robert had gone underground where Tiffany had come out.

Algy knew of three openings to the passages, but he knew nothing beyond that; his people had had no portable light when they'd lived in the *greenplace,* and the dark holes in the earth there had never been entered voluntarily, since those who had fallen in had tended never to return. They tried all three openings until they found a passage leading into the hill.

Genie's lantern shone on wet, slimy walls, and, before long, the passageway's floor gave way to a yellowish, fungal muck that Genie might have turned back from if not for his mounting excitement: They walked in an ancient hallway; in places, chips of tiling still clung tenuously to the walls. They reached an intersection at the end of the hall; two of the branches proved to be water-filled stairwells. They took the remaining branch, a dry corridor, and continued.

Caverns—rooms—began to open up on either side. In many, the roots of the trees above dangled freely from the ceilings; rot and decay filled the air, and several times Genie felt glass crunching beneath his feet. In one room they found row upon row of three-foot-high metal half spheres that looked like giant cups where the hanging roots gathered and curled around themselves. Piles of huge test tubes littered the floor around the cups.

In a room beyond, up a short flight of stairs, they found skeletons, many still covered with strips of petrified, rock-hard flesh, skeletons from rodent to human. It was there that Genie found the final piece of his puzzle: Bolted into the old wall, next to the doorway, was a plaque that read: DANGER! TESTING AREA—ATMOSPHERE TOXIC. Beneath the wording he found a symbol he'd seen once before, on a (mysteriously empty) file folder in the Grant T & E archives.

He'd taken his assignment with the Grants in 2075. In 2079—in June, if he remembered correctly—they'd awakened him in the middle of the night and sent him to Australia with Tiffany, Robert, and Rachel to play bodyguard with but one explicit instruction: to keep them there and occupied for at least a month. Upon his return, he'd managed to learn only that there had been some sort of disaster and that the few people who knew anything about it weren't talking. He hadn't asked questions. A couple of years later, during an industrial espionage alert when he'd found himself guarding the archives vault, he'd noticed an open file cabinet, gone to close it, and fallen victim to curiosity for the first time in many years. Inside the cabinet, in the most of the folders, he'd found reams of papers covered with minute legal gibberish: contracts, patent applications, and corporate classification guidelines that he didn't even attempt to understand (especially when his every nerve felt on fire, screaming for him to hurry up and close the drawer). But he'd found the one empty folder, and he'd remembered it because every other folder had been *packed* with documents. The only thing on the one had been the symbol, a triangle filled with a weirdly stylized equation of some sort.

He'd shut the drawer but remembered the symbol. Outside the room with the skeletons, he and Algy found the symbol again in three other places before they left. All the while, Genie felt sure he'd learned the *answer* (and, in fact, he'd learned it first, even before Mother Grant). About that file cabinet, that day in the archives, he'd understood only one thing with certainty: the label stuck on the front. It had read, simply, BIOLOGICAL/GENETIC ENGINEERING.

When they'd regained the fresh air of the *greenplace*, Genie looked at Algy's kind, inquisitive face and burst into an uncontrollable fit of laughter. Somehow he *knew* he looked at an unexpected by-product of that disaster of June 2079. It was impossible that Algy could be a child of the last—the definitive—nuclear war. It was impossible that Algy and his people had evolved randomly from normal human stock. Somehow the Grant family, in its experimental zeal, its lust for immortality and invulnerability and God-only-knew what else, had given birth to its own downfall. That nameless project had fully backfired, in spite of whatever the Grants had done in attempting to obliterate it.

They'd tried, at the least, to bury it. Looking around, Genie grew more certain (and more euphoric at the convolutions of irony) that this was the place he'd shared that last day with Crystal. The hill itself then, in 2085, would have been treeless, covered only with grass.

"Did you know, Daniel, that I'd never even heard of that place Genie found? Genie told Jan all about it, that last afternoon, when we were all back in the cage. Jan hadn't heard of it either. . . .

"The company did other things, though, that we all knew about. Definitely—terrible things. If there's one thing good about all this, it's that you'll never have to know your great-grandmother. I'm not sure the world ever had to put up with a more self-centered, heartless, evil bitch. . . ."

V.

"What?!" Philip spat into the communipact.

"We captured one last night."

"Christ! They're all out looking for him. Robert was with him!"

"Uh—"

"What ?"

Silence.

Philip shook the communipact, muttering under his breath and looking over at Martin and Madonna who, as always, were tangled together asleep. They'd kept him up half the night with their grunting and moaning; they thought he never heard them, but he did. Then they slept all through the day, expecting him to wake them when Tiffany or Jan brought food and water. He was sick of it, sick of them, sick of everything. And now Mother Grant had gone and done it without even letting him know ahead of time.

He could have worked it out, planned it right himself. He'd almost had Tiffany on his side that afternoon, when she'd come to bring their water and food and apologize for leaving them with nothing the day before. He could see it in her eyes; he'd almost had her! Then he could have planned it right, but no, they obviously weren't going to let that happen. They weren't going to let Philip call the shots, not he who had suffered through all this bullshit to make sure they did it right!

"Philip!"

Mother Grant's voice.

"Yes, Mother," he said wearily into the communipact. *Here it comes. . . .*

"Robert's dead."

"What?!"

"He got in the way, love. It was an accident, honest."

"They're tracking them, Mother. They've got that god-damned superdog now, and they're tracking them."

"Don't worry, sonny. Everything's under control. Sit tight—Complex One out."

Like hell, he thought, trying to quell his rage.

Goddamn wonderdog! Gonna figure something out sure as shit, then we'll all be in it! Tiffany, Jan—everybody back in the cage. . . . They'll find the 'pact, or someone will tell them. Tiffany or Martin, and it'll be my ass they take apart. My ass!

Martin and Madonna still slept. Out of the shade it was hot, but not unbearably so. Philip looked cautiously out the window of the shelter; there was no one in sight except the one who was supposed to be guarding him. Nervously, he crept out and looked in every direction—still no one; they were all looking for Robert and Stick or whatever his name was.

Now was his only chance.

Philip inched toward the gap in the wire, stepped gingerly over the sleeping guard, and raced for cover.

Now what?

He dodged aimlessly from building to building until he realized, in fact, that some were occupied, some housed sleepers, refugees from the sun. He looked up; they would soon wake as the siesta hours came to a close. And the others would be back.

He picked a direction at random and ran, in a crouch, away from the encampment.

The sun beat down on his back and neck. He'd already thrown away his shirt in an attempt to keep cool; why had he done something so stupid?

Just then he spied an outcrop and sought its shade.

Underground.

That's where he hid, and just in time, too. He could hear voices and shuffling footsteps—lots of them—beyond the cave's mouth.

The big black mutant bellowed mournfully, out there under the sun.

The cave was cool.

Someone was crying.

He heard no laughter.

Growls from the wonderdog.

More bellowing.

Philip slid farther down into the darkness.

Near the end, he wandered blindly. Perhaps he thought desperate thoughts: how to get out, how to turn back, how to reach that river . . . what were those sounds? Perhaps he kept plotting revenge: In his mind, he could make the monsters vulnerable; in his dreams, he had torn their hearts out and held them before their eyes before they died. In his dreams, he had dreamed himself the torturer, the vindicator, the emperor.

But he walked in darkness and had no magic lantern to protect him. The dark creatures, whatever they were, found him, and they attacked.

Philip managed a few screams, a few nightmarish wails, and even a coherent sentence or two into the communipact before he died. Within the hour, Fender Fang led Monk to the bloody pile of bones the dark creatures left behind.

VI.

". . . they're eating me!"

Madeline tapped her fingers impatiently against the arm of her chair. "For goodness sakes, boy, calm down!"

"Mother!"

"Philip, what are you on about?

"Philip?"

"I'm sorry, Mother," Medusa piped in softly, "but the transmission was disrupted. I cannot maintain contact."

"What happened?"

"Insufficient data. Stress factors in his voice suggested extreme levels of pain."

"They wouldn't have tortured him with the 'pact in his hand."

"Perhaps he escaped. His signal strength was significantly weaker than normal, and triangulation data indicate that he transmitted from a location some five hundred fifteen meters from his usual point of contact—"

"Escaped!"

"—give or take two point three meters. Yes."

"The damned *fool*! We needed him! Where's Martin? Was he with him?"

"Insufficient data."

"*Shit!* Robert! Come here, boy. I think you've lost another nephew."

Robert Travis Grant III approached Madeline and laid a hand on hers. "I know, Mother. Calm down, please. You don't want to strain your heart."

"But . . ." she sputtered, banging on the arm of her chair. "*Shit!* Philip! Idiot! I always knew you were an idiot! Why am I surrounded by idiots?"

"I'm here," Robert Travis insisted softly. "I'm not an idiot. I have your intelligence; you've said so before."

"I know, son. But we needed that little bastard, didn't we? And why in hell haven't we heard from the goddamn lab?"

"I don't know, Mother. Medusa?"

"No relevant data, Master Grant."

Madeline Grant looked up at her son. "Gotta do everything around here, don't we? Let's go put some fire under their asses!"

Robert Travis nodded and grasped the arm of her chair. "I'll steer," he said as she flipped a switch and the chair's hoverjets kicked in.

Madeline Grant could still walk, but she preferred to float. Seated, she felt she maintained her dignity at all times.

They'd strapped Stigg to a table and done their best to cut into him. Lasers failed, scalpels broke, and one biotech lay in a bed in the infirmary beyond, wounded in the stomach by a high-speed tungsten bullet that had barely dented Stigg's chest and then bounced off and all around the room. It was as if Stigg's skin got tougher, not weaker, in his vulnerability.

For the moment, they'd had to settle for tissue scrapings from his eyes.

When Madeline breezed into the room, work ceased. One by one, the biotechs moved away from Stigg. Three others, who sat at terminals linked into their diagnostic expert systems, slowly grew aware of the inactivity and turned in their chairs, fidgeting nervously in their seats against the impulse to rise and stand at attention.

"Well?" Madeline asked impatiently, staring at one of the seated men, the chief biotech, a man of fifty who'd worked for the Grants since he was fifteen.

He rose, looking at the other technicians for some sign of a significant breakthrough. Their eyes fell, in unison, to the floor. He cleared his throat.

"MD49, ma'am. That's all we know so far."

"MD49? What's that?"

"We don't really understand that, either. Medusa gave us the data."

"Go on."

"You told Medusa to help us if she could, didn't you?"

"Yes."

"Well, we scratched our heads over the data, gave it to Medusa, and she gave us some DNA maps labeled MD49."

"Medusa?"

"Yes, Mother Grant."

"Give me some help, please. What the hell's he talking about?"

"Security-controlled data."

"Override."

"MD49 DNA configurations roughly matched the configurations I was provided. Circumstance mandated download of match-related data."

"And?"

"Project X-3. DNA-enhanced molecular bonding stimulated into active mutation. Project canceled by chief technicians for undocumented reasons."

"One of our projects?"

"Yes, Mother Grant. Terminated in twenty seventy-nine."

"Oh, yes—I remember now. What does this mean?"

"It means," the biotech said, "that that thing on the table is all but invincible, possibly immortal as well. Your project succeeded."

"Well, that won't do at all," she said, her fierce eyes darting around the room and resting, finally, on her son. "Only one option left. Right Robert?"

"You know best, Mother."

"Good." She looked at the biotech, then glanced at the table where Stigg lay motionless. "We're going to have to nuke the bastards."

VII.

Until Martin grabbed Tiffany and shook her, she heard no one, felt only heartwrenching anguish, and saw only Robert's body with its coat of light brown dirt and the darker, redder brown of his chest. Even when she opened her eyes, the image wouldn't go away, as if her mind, presented with yet another vision of death, fixed on it and clung to it, refusing to assimilate the illusory, time-based movements of the living around her. Death was Robert; Robert death —he was younger than she; she could remember his infancy, his childhood, his first lost tooth, his sixteenth birthday. . . . And now he was done. For him, the world had stopped, and for a time, Tiffany's world stopped with her realization of the end of his.

They pushed her, dragged her, and carried her back to throw her and her people back in their cage with Martin and Madonna. She was aware of nothing; she could not hear the menacing growls rumbling deep in Fender Fang's throat. She could not see the dark, animal rage that had transformed the deep blues of Monk's eyes into something feral, inhuman.

Rachel could. She'd stood next to Monk while he'd learned of Robert's death and while Fender showed them all where Stigg's scent disappeared. She'd stood next to Monk while Fender scouted in all directions, finally discovering the faint metallic trail left by the battle droid as it had labored to stay airborne under Stigg's immense weight. Rachel had watched Monk transform as he'd pieced together the evidence and realized that some ancients remained free and hostile. It didn't matter that they'd killed one of their own; that only proved to him the survival of their evil, their diseases of murder, war, and treachery. Rachel had witnessed the dawning of all these thoughts, and she'd felt the back of his hand as she'd tried, in spite of it all, to cling to him.

He'd cast her aside, though. Forever.

Genie cursed. He and Algy watched the procession from a distance. Two of Monk's larger males, warrior types, had started out to intercept them, to welcome their return from the *greenplace*.

Something had happened, Genie realized. Something had happened, and now everything was going to change—he *knew* it. Had they found Robert? Just that—what else? Nothing good, he supposed. . . .

So much for his discovery. His knowledge, and his dreams. He wondered whether he should run now, escape if he could, but one look into Algy's eyes left him shattered inside, unable even to think clearly. The old mutant was guessing, too. Genie saw the pain there in his eyes, a sense of betrayal, so deep it couldn't even accuse. Raw pain, eyes like windows into a child's hell, wounds on an innocent soul.

What had happened?

"Battle droid," Jan whispered to him softly after Monk's men had taken him from Algy's side and thrown him among his own people, among the ancients.

Mother Grant! . . .

He'd been a fool! He'd all but forgotten her, wished her away like a bad memory, sure she would look out, see the state of the world, and return to sleep, like a groundhog, emerging, seeing its shadow, and retreating back into hibernation. What could she possibly imagine doing against *this*? Was she stupid? Did the arrogant old witch really think she could *win*?

He couldn't believe it. Even after the mutants threw them—all of them—back into Philip's cage, he still couldn't believe it.

And then Philip wasn't there, anywhere among them. The little bastard had been behind this, too, Genie thought. If he came back, Genie was going to wring his neck. . . . *Goddamnit! Why didn't you think? Why didn't you expect this?*

What can you do now?

He grew nervous, made his way to the perimeter of the cage, and squeezed the wire in his hands. He'd forgotten to pay attention. For how long? What were they doing now? All of them gathered in a group, about forty meters away. Genie watched. Monk and Fender came out of the desert at the edge of his vision, loping across the dirt. Fender carried—something in his mouth.

Genie watched, time passing like slow thunder inside his head. The group split suddenly, Algy and a few others coming toward him, the rest, led by Monk, racing off for the horizon.

Algy now held the something—a tattered red rag—in his hand. The other three split off, posting themselves around the cage. Genie kept coming.

"A piece of your Philip," Algy said, tossing the rag into the wire. It hung there, next to Genie's hand. "Don't worry, Fender didn't do it. They found him, what little that was left."

"I didn't know, Algy," Genie pleaded.

The old mutant ignored him. "Monk's gone to find where the new robot came from."

Those wounded eyes . . . "You're not going with him?"

"No," Algy said after a long silence. "Back to the drawing board, as you people used to say. I need to be alone, to think."

"I didn't know, Algy!"

"Maybe you should have." He turned his back. He left. *Maybe you should have.* . . .

But Genie had known. He'd lied. He'd known, but refused to remember.

"Tiffany?" Jan said softly.

Tiffany opened her eyes, looked past Jan, and screamed.

Martin pushed Jan out of the way and grabbed Tiffany's shoulders. "Tiffany!" he growled under her screams. "Shut up!" He slapped her violently and she fell to the floor; then he felt his own body whirling around, and iron fingers gripped his neck.

"Leggo," he sputtered.

"Touch her again"—Genie snarled—"and I'll kill you."

"Leggo!" He could barely hear his own voice.

Genie shifted his grip to the inside of Martin's shoulder. "Can you breathe now?"

Martin swallowed and nodded.

"Good. You don't touch her. You don't touch anybody."

Martin glanced down at Tiffany. She watched them dully; she'd stopped screaming, and something in her eyes proved her marginally aware of her surroundings.

"It worked," Martin protested. "She snapped out of it!"

"I don't care if you sent her to heaven and back! You're a fucking idiot! You and that shit-for-brains cousin of yours blew everything! Couldn't you see what we had here? No?

203

You're ready to die now, I suppose? Those three,'' he said, nodding his head toward their guards, "could tear all of us limb from limb and never break a sweat!''

"They're not human! They probably don't know how to sweat. We can escape now!''

"Oh, yeah?'' Genie let go of him and nudged him back. "Go ahead. Lead the charge.''

Martin looked around nervously, but he didn't move.

Genie smiled sadly. "I didn't think so,'' he spat, glaring at Martin until the other man moved nervously away.

VIII.

". . . yeah, Daniel, terrible things she did, your great-grandmother. Even in the little things, she twisted men's souls. You know that biotech? The one who told her about the MD49? Half the time, she acted like she hardly knew him, but he'd been around for years, ever since I could remember. Name was Henry Blakely, but we called him 'the hatchet moron.' God, the things it was rumored he'd done for her! All out of some twisted idea of love or something; everybody knew it, he was one of those people whose whole life story sat there, visible to everyone, in his face. . . . The love, the heartless love she'd inflicted upon him like a curse. She used him for anything, brainwashing, torture, you name it. He did it, no matter what, even though he didn't seem a particularly cruel man. And I wonder whether he was thinking of anything but pleasing her, the whole time he worked.

"But Stigg—the poor mad doctor couldn't do anything with him, the way he kept getting tougher the more they tried to stick him. It's really quite funny if you think about it. . . ."

* * *

In the end, they took Stigg back to the surface, hoping he'd make a beeline back to his home. They propped him up, pointed him in the right direction, and when he started to wake, his legs took it from there.

Madeline Grant watched, gleefully. She was aware of Monk's approach, and all her sensors indicated that Monk and Stigg would cross paths just exactly where she wanted them. The perfection of it all made her feel positively young again.

Monk met Stigg five miles from Complex One, some twelve or thirteen miles from the Batcave. No one knows what they said during those few brief minutes before hell broke loose. No one knows whether Stigg remembered anything that had happened to him, or whether it darkened Monk's mood even deeper.

Then came the high, shrieking whistle, followed by hell. What Monk must have felt during those moments. . . . The roar of annihilated matter against his skin, the incredible, indescribable heat, the smell of his instantly incinerated hair, the blast of wind that lifted him high off the earth only to throw him back, pummeling him with boulders, pelting him with sand, smashing his body against molten earth, glass now, forged in a heat that mankind had stolen from the stars. The roar . . . through the flames, the screams of those weaker, their melting flesh, the death in their eyes.

The fires of the ancients, scorching the earth anew.

He didn't know how many had survived; he could only count how many came staggering out of the dust while he watched the sky above grow dark with cloud and blot out the sun. Stigg came out of the dust. Fender Fang followed. Part of Monk must have wanted to search through the rubble for the rest of them, but another part, a stronger part, seethed with a fury as indescribable as that which had fallen from the heavens upon their heads.

With his army now of only three, Monk continued on.

"Shit," Genie whispered as the thunder faded and the world grew so silent that even the wind didn't speak. No one moved; everyone remained frozen, their eyes fixed on the slow, horrible blossoming of the mushroom cloud on the horizon.

The *whoosh* of approaching hovercraft, when it came, sounded unreal, impossible after that shattering thunder. But the craft came, the first within ten yards of their guard before veering off. The mutants, stunned suddenly into action, raced after it. The second craft came and settled outside the cage. Before Genie could force his body into action, Martin had passed him, Madonna on one side, Tiffany dragging along behind him.

Elison Grant jumped out of the hovercraft and moved to help Martin get the women aboard. "Move!" he shouted back at the others.

No one did; most eyes remained fixed on the distant cloud in the sky. They hadn't seen the final end of humanity. They hadn't lived through it; they'd only come to understand it through the fact that humanity as they'd known it was gone. Now the visual, concrete manifestation, the ghost of the nightly vidnews, struck home. No longer did it blossom over Africa, Asia, Latin America, California. It had risen, real, before their eyes, as terrible in its symmetry and serene beauty as the Second Coming of an angry Christ. No one among them had failed to fear it, to imagine it countless times over and shudder at thoughts of its indiscriminate power, its destructive wrath.

Rachel faced the terrible phantom, realization mushrooming up her spine as surely as the pillar of death—the billowing, living headstone of the man she loved—had risen from the distant earth. *Monk!* she thought. . . . Her mouth fell open, frozen in midwhisper, and her dreams decayed and crumbled behind her eyes. Within her, everything stopped. She became a shell, lifeless, thoughtless, full of a mourning so deep that she shut it off from her and made herself numb.

Jan glanced at her father and hated and loved him at the same time. *He* had done this, he and his kind. But she felt so small before it all, and in her smallness he was still her father, the strong man with the gentle voice; the protective arms; the sure, assuring eyes. Nothing was black and white; nothing was good or evil at that moment, not even within herself. *"They've forgotten us,"* she'd told Tiffany, practically begged Tiffany. Never. Never . . .

"Do what you want," Genie said next to her. "I'm staying, for what it's worth."

Nothing. Even what might have been is lost now. Stay or go? she wondered. Either path was madness. Where was her third choice? What life did either choice offer? She wanted to go home! She wanted to be back in the city, with her apartment, her job, and her weekends in London or Toronto. . . . Home—her sisters . . . Ironically, Martin had already decided for her; Martin, who had snuck Tiffany past them all. If she stayed, she'd be abandoning Tiffany to *them*, leaving her to face them alone.

Stiff-lipped, she reached for Rachel's hand and pulled, struggling out to the hovercraft; her sister offered little resistance. Elison Grant—her father—lifted her in his strong arms and placed her inside.

As they sped away, Jan looked back to Genie and saw him leading his men out of the cage and across to the Batcave where, she assumed, it would be safer when the fallout came.

That was the last anyone saw of Philip's militia and its leader.

IX.

"Whahoooh!" came Robert Travis's voice through Medusa's audcircuits.

On the vidscreen, they could see him at the bottom, in the front of the hovercraft in his silver suit, flanked by two silver men carrying shoulder-held ground-to-ground missiles.

Madeline chuckled.

Mason Grant, her eldest son, stood next to her. "Don't you think this is getting a little carried away, Mother?"

"Nonsense!" she declared, never looking away from the screen. "The boy's perfectly protected from any radiation, and he is, after all, a boy. This is an educational experience. Besides," she added, chuckling again, "don't think I've forgotten your fleet of sportsflyers and your joyrides when you were his age. You'd deny the same fun to him now, just because you're older, more boring, and think you know better? He'll never have the same opportunities you had, Mason. You should feel sorry for him. Loosen up, relive your childhood or something."

"What about the firestorm?"

"What firestorm? There's nothing out there to burn, you silly fool. The heat has passed."

Mason fell silent and watched his little brother. He felt silly thinking of Robert Travis as his brother; he always did, especially when his own son was thirty years older than his youngest brother. He suspected that his mother had taken particular pleasure in cheating Nature so long after her menopause. But with science that could preserve adult humans over thousands of years, how difficult could it have been to keep an egg and sperm vital over decades?

Through the vidscreen, Mason felt the exhilaration of Robert Travis's ride; the vidlens, mounted high in the rear of the hovercraft, gave them a sweeping view of the awesomely desolate landscape. A glittery haze, like a mirage, sprung up in the distance as the craft sped toward to the site of the blast.

"Don't let him get too close to that," Mason said. "I don't care how safe you think it is."

"Don't worry—" Madeline started, then she gasped. The picture on the vidscreen tumbled.

They'd all seen a flash of movement, a hulking, black figure rising up in the hovercraft's path. For a second, his face had filled the screen—a fierce face, blackened, charred, hairless. He'd stopped the craft momentarily, and three silver bodies had shot ahead, still traveling at a couple of hundred kilometers per hour.

Then the screen had tumbled as the rear of the craft lifted up and went end over end after its passengers.

"Robert!" Madeline shrieked, feeling the fingers of her eldest digging into her shoulder. *"Robert!"*

"Life functions terminated on impact, Mother Grant," Medusa said. "He will not answer."

The hovercraft settled; amazingly, the vidlens survived. They saw the black giant approach, followed by a horrible, snarling, hairless beast that almost looked like a dog. Behind them came something that looked like the orange man they'd captured. Except his skin was black, and charred like the others'. In the distant haze over the blast site—there seemed to be movement there as well.

"Jesus Christ," Mason exclaimed softly. "They survived even that."

Madeline, frozen stiff, cleared her throat. For a moment, Mason thought she'd cried; if she had, it would've been the first time he'd ever heard it. But no, when her voice came, it came clear and firm.

"Ready that starship," she said. "This is hell. It isn't Earth anymore."

Mason breathed a sigh of relief. He'd half-expected her to order another nuclear attack.

Actually, she almost had. "I'm not running from a fight," she added. "I'm cheating them of victory."

She looked up into his eyes. "Get everything ready, son," she said. "Go. Leave me alone with my thoughts for a while."

Mason nodded and left the room.

X.

Staring at the huge cloud to her left, its dirty whiteness and wispy stem, Tiffany slowly realized what must have happened.

It had all happened so fast, once they'd discovered Robert's buried body. Philip had died; she had brothers no longer, but the day before, she'd had two. One like a child in a playground; the other, equally a child, caged by self-imposed misery and pride. He had killed them, Tiffany thought. He'd killed them all, just as she and Jan had feared.

Over there, to her left, the evil of the past had been reborn.

But no—it wasn't really Philip's fault. It couldn't be, just as surely as it couldn't really be hers, even though she'd started it all. Neither of them had had control over things. All the tragedies—they were the mistakes men were doomed from the start to make. No single one of them could have stopped any of it. Individuals, she thought, were like single pebbles, powerless to fight or turn back the ongoing, eternal avalanche that carried them all down, to be buried in darkness.

So history revealed.

Another phantom from the past rose up on the horizon ahead—the silvery pillar of a starship. She'd been right: Mother Grant had thought of everything. As they sped toward it, Tiffany resisted an absurd impulse to laugh. All this! she thought. All this—all this only to leave it behind, to keep running from a past that refused to allow escape. Out to the stars now, the unsure escape taken by so many others during her century. Where had they gone? Would she learn now? Would she learn that even among the stars there was no escape?

It seemed like a dream again: the starship, already airborne on top of the magnetic pillow over its launchpad, the hovercraft dropping them right next to the liftshaft, their rapid ascent on the metal platform, their single-file entrance into their new time capsule. No one was speaking; no one dared to challenge the gravity of events with mere words.

They all went, eventually, to the main viewport, sharing an unspoken desire to see the last of their planet, no matter how desolate, how barren, it had become.

They were on, Tiffany realized, the thirteenth exodus ship, the first after the twelve that had gone before Sub-Space Corporation's collapse. She sensed something significant in the number; it dredged up hilarious parallels, hesitant memories—from *Battlestar Galactica?* From the

Bible? From humanity's myth itself, the ancient mystical numbers: three, seven, nine, and thirteen. The high number, the baker's dozen.

The number of uncertain luck.

The last tragedy fell upon Mother Grant herself.

Monk failed to understand the starship's significance until the last moment, and attacked instead the surface gate into the cryocomplex.

Unlike his earlier assault on Complex Two, he smashed down this door in one terrible blow. Fender Fang and Stigg followed him in.

Madeline, alone in her misery, didn't have time to reach the starship. They caught her in the halls. Upon her body, Fender Fang unleashed all his fury and heartache.

She didn't live long.

Medusa reported the incident to Mason Grant as she off-loaded her critical systems into the ship.

Monk, Fender, and Stigg emerged from the depths of Complex One. With a few other, unrecognizable survivors who had straggled to the scene, they gathered around the starship that hovered twenty feet over their heads. Monk, for unknown reasons, now held the inert husk of a battle droid in his arms.

At first sight of him, Rachel screamed and tried to run for the exit; her father caught her and quickly had a biotech inject her with enough sedative to keep her meek for days.

The moment the computers announced readiness for launch, Mason gave the order. Thunder erupted from the ship's engines. For a moment, nothing happened; then hell exploded, once again erupting to consume the mutants in a nuclear fire easily as hot as the first.

Tiffany watched Monk. As the flames shot out, he jumped back and heaved the battle droid at the ship. That last attack damaged certain systems in the starship's subspace drive that would take years to repair. But it didn't stop the liftoff; it didn't avert the nuclear hell.

The bright fires consumed Monk; Tiffany watched until the polarizers in the viewers turned everything black, and the starship roared upward, into the sky.

She shuddered, closing her eyes. There, she could see him alive. She saw him as she'd seen him first, on the stage of the Batcave, bathed in white light, his voice making her ache inside, and his deep blue eyes piercing through hers, to her soul.

"All might have turned out well, Daniel. I mean, at first they pumped so many drugs into us that we might have believed anything, that it was one long crazy nightmare or something. But we—your aunts and I—started getting bigger, and things just got worse.

"Jan nearly went insane, thinking she was going to bear the child of her dead brother. But we did DNA scans and found MD49 in the fetus. So it was someone else—David's father. No idea who, though. . . .

"Rachel probably conceived after Jan, after that night of the feast, since Mark, Marsha, and Diane were born last of all of you, and I guess I was the first, wasn't I? That day in Eden, you know, with Stigg . . . when I was trying to make the dream go away . . ."

Chapter

· 6 ·

■ THE END, Daniel thought as he instructed his sphere to print out copies of the last few pages to send to the others.

He'd been sending out the story, a few pages at a time, his writing interspersed with days, weeks of brooding.

The end. It hadn't been easy to write; it hadn't, he supposed, been easy for the others to read. The end for which they'd waited so long, so terrible, so swift and brief, like a knife into their hearts. He was glad he'd saved it, that he'd taken so long, making them wait and wonder and laugh and cry at small heartaches, small and insignificant in contrast to the end, which he alone had harbored, had reflected upon, had tried to understand. It still made little sense; and now, instead of hurting less, it hurt more, as if he'd made it more real by writing it, as if all the while he'd written, before he'd finished, he'd possessed some sort of subtle, intangible power to change things, to make things different, brighter, full of some hope for them, for the Earth itself.

No hope now. With his last words, his hopes had deflated like balloons. He felt a desert inside, an uncaring, featureless void where disturbing, molasses-slow nightmares hid under invisible rocks, where the safest action was inaction, where the most meaningful thought was no thought at all.

Where time stopped and eternity opened up, split by the last cries of a dead race returning to vomit up all its horrors, to fill the void with its fears and its crimes. His void.

All that malignancy, festering now inside himself.

The first reaction came from David, David's first message to anyone in a week. It read:

I am dead already
I have dreamed the dream of nothing and know it is mine
It is me, and I know the dark
I know a black blacker than space

I am a ghost already
My flesh lies
Caging me
As if I were alive to feel the sun
But I know illusion
And I know where it hides
In my mind.

They were ten days from Earthfall. The planet was blue and brown and white: no green, at least not from a distance.

David saw his death coming ever more near—he would fly by Earth and then burn as his orbit decayed, ever more near to the sun. He had offered Daniel a taste of his death in exchange for Daniel's ending. It was fitting, Daniel thought. Death for death.

* * *

Monica's reply came next. She wrote, simply, *That's all?*

That's all. . . . Truly, he thought—there was more real, solid truth in the end of the story than anywhere else. He hadn't elaborated, overanalyzed, tried to explore the depraved, wretched mind of his great-grandmother or tried to cloak events with a sheen of unreal poetry. Stark had been Tiffany's words of her grandmother and Henry Blakely, the hatchet moron. Stark had been Madeline Grant's conversations (guaranteed accurate because Tiffany had found recordings of them in Medusa's disabled memory banks). Stark—Daniel had left it all stark. Stark like death. Elaboration could never have deflected, or changed the power, of those last, fateful events.

No, Daniel wrote Monica back finally, *then came us. We grew, and they hated us because they hated what we were. Our mothers sent us back out into space, back to Earth, to save our lives. They wanted to kill us.*

Martin died, Monica replied. *Tiffany shot him before they sent us out into space. For ages, I thought that memory a dream, but I'm sure now it was real. Don't you remember?*

Yes, he wrote, *the dead man on the floor before we left. How are you sure it was Martin?*

It had to be, she answered. *He had to die. Before everything ended, he had to die. In fact, they all should have died, everyone except Tiffany, Rachel, and Jan.*

Maybe they did, Daniel wrote, ending the exchange. *We'll never know, will we?*

Diane wrote nothing for two days, but when she wrote, she made no mention at all of Tiffany's story.

She renewed their hope with a simple question, one that made them forget the tragedies of the past and see, suddenly, the brightness and wonder and promise of the future. She did all this with one simple question:

217

Hey, she wrote to each of them, *have any of you ever hurt yourself—with a cut or a bruise or anything—in the last few years?*

No, Daniel realized, he hadn't. Not since he'd banged up his head dodging asteroids, when Mark and Marsha had died. If he dug his fingernails into his skin, he left no mark. If he banged his head as hard as he could against his desk, he left no bruise.

No, he wrote back excitedly, *I haven't, but the important question is whether David has.*

He says he hasn't either, came Diane's reply.

"How big a thing," Daniel asked his sphere, "can you take in from space?"

"What do you mean?"

"Could you bring a person inside, a person my size?"

"Probably. Are you going outside the sphere, Daniel? That is not a wise idea. You cannot breathe in space."

"I know that. But I could hold my breath."

"You would still die. Your body would explode with no atmospheric pressure on the skin."

"Even if I have very tough skin?"

"You would still explode. It might take longer."

They talked David into trying it two days later. They had his sphere make sheets of tough plastic, just in case, and David wrapped up his body in the stuff before ordering his sphere to inject him into the void.

He came to Daniel's sphere, since Daniel's was the closest.

They all watched—all held their own breath—during David's two-minute trip. They watched him in his glittering, spinning cocoon. They held their breath until he collided with the soft black panel on the hull of Daniel's sphere.

The sphere passed the cocoon inside. Daniel still didn't

breathe. Frantically, he tore the plastic away from David's body, from his face. David's eyes were closed, his face unmoving.

"David!" Daniel said, touching the face. "David! Please! Be alive!"

Slowly, Daniel's cousin smiled, a weak, unsure smile, a smile he hadn't smiled in two years. *I'm alive,* he said with his smile.

He opened his eyes.

Chapter

·7·

■ THEY TALKED FOR DAYS, sleeping only when they collapsed from happy exhaustion. They talked about everything, anything, silly things like how it felt to have the whiskers that now pushed through their cheeks and chins, and how it felt when you held your breath, pinched your nose, and tried like hell to breathe out.

They'd stand side by side for hours, looking at each other and their warped reflections on the inside surface of the sphere, looking at each other's body and comparing, inch by inch, the similarities and differences. They decided they looked like brothers.

The only things they really didn't talk about much were Tiffany's story and David's own, depressed poetry. When Daniel brought up the latter, David said, "Oh, that. I was lonely—forget it."

They also watched vid, showing each other's favorites (Daniel's were *Merry Christmas, Mr. Lawrence*, *The Lost*

History of Kate McCloud, and *Emergence.* David's were *Suicide Shift, Marooned,* and *The Wall).* Daniel loved David's first and last and thought it remarkable that he'd never watched them on his own. He didn't care much for *Marooned,* but he could understand why David liked it.

In between the vids and the talking, they did their best to answer all the questions sent by the girls. That was hard: It was very hard to be having fun when they knew that Monica and Diane fell deeper and deeper into solitary depressions just because they knew Daniel and David were together. Diane even suggested that she and Monica do the same thing David had done, and then they could all ride to Earth's surface in the same sphere. *No,* Daniel told her sadly. They shouldn't take that risk again. Besides, the reason they'd each been alone in the first place was to keep them from all dying together. The spheres weren't perfect; they'd lost two already. On top of that, Daniel's sphere might strain with too much weight inside.

They didn't have long to wait, anyway. Only a couple of days.

Earth, he told the girls, was large and beautiful next to its moon. *Watch it,* he wrote. *We'll all be together soon enough.*

They gained on the planet, the spheres' thrusters kicking in, establishing an orbit around Earth. David's sphere shot away from them then. Daniel and David watched it disappear rapidly from sight. They held hands; David weeped, both in joy and sadness. His sphere, indeed, had been a friend. As Daniel thought about it, he realized that he would hate to leave his own sphere. He knew it was a computer, that it was lifeless, but in his heart, it just didn't feel that way.

Monica changed the subject then by asking whether they ought to have their spheres generate new clothes. One by one, over the past years as they'd neared the sun and their environment had grown warmer, they'd each given up the ancient custom. Monica's question caused a few giggles, and it helped David get over the loss of his sphere. In the end, after a short debate during which Diane joked that they'd surely, no matter what, be out of fashion, they voted against it.

After that was over, Diane informed them that her sphere was mapping the planet. She'd written the program long ago. She was very excited; the sphere kept finding small, disparate patches of green, things she couldn't see with her own eyes, but the sphere swore they were there. There was still life on Earth in places. Maybe not *human* life, but definitely life. She asked Daniel whether they should allow the spheres to continue on their programmed descent vectors, which would land them near the place from which their mothers had left, or whether they should reprogram to land near one of the larger patches of green elsewhere on the planet.

Daniel toyed with that question, and avoided answering it, for a long time. In the end, he wrote Diane, *We have to know. I know why you ask, because the greenplace there does not make good food, and because we may die if we find no way to eat. But we have to know. We have to know what our mothers left behind. We have to hope. We saved David; maybe there's more hope left. Besides, Algy should still be alive. . . .*

Reluctantly, Diane agreed.

The descent was breathtaking, scary, and totally out of their control. They landed on, and skidded across, water—the Atlantic Ocean. When they came to rest, the spheres immediately propelled them over the waves westward, to the land once known as America.

It took several hours, hours full of impatience, and hours

of bone-wrenching pain. Though they'd known gravity, they'd never known their bodies to be *so* heavy. It was effort enough to stand, but they *had* to stand to see out of their spheres, to see where they were going, to see each other so close, scarcely meters away. Monica *was* beautiful. So was Diane, and she had dark, olive skin, a mysterious blend of Rachel's pale white and Monk's obsidian black.

In time, they reached a white, sandy beach and the spheres spilled them out onto the sands. Naked, they stood, seeing each other for the first time.

Daniel ran, stumbling, falling, fighting the new gravity, until he fell into Monica's open arms. David ran next to him to embrace Diane. The four of them came together then and fell, in an unruly heap, onto the beach. There, exhausted and reveling in the new sensations of skin against skin, they slept.

When they woke it was morning, and their spheres had floated off, now mere dots on the blue horizon. They had nowhere to go but inland.

They walked, their progress excruciatingly slow. They'd learned already that things were not always as they seemed: The ocean water was not like the water of the spheres; it made them gag and choke. It made them *more* thirsty, not less.

By the end of the first day of slow walking, they had found no river or stream or pond or spring, and Daniel began to wonder whether they would die. In all of their faces, he saw pain; the agonies of Earth's gravity and Earth's heat made them lifeless, stealing away the joy of their reunion. When he looked at Monica, and she at him, he wanted to cry, to hug her, but touching made them hurt. Every movement made them hurt.

They gave up on walking near sunset, collapsed to the ground, and slept again.

* * *

Dawn brought rain and rekindled hope.

The water came from the sky, cool and wet on their sleeping bodies. Daniel woke when it first splashed on his cheek. He looked up at the dark clouds above, then a drop hit his forehead, another hit his chest, and he thought, *Rain! Real, Earth—life-giving—rain!*

It came faster. He licked it from his hands and arms, tasting Earth water for the first time, a taste more unique, equally as powerful, as the gin he'd asked his sphere to manufacture. He shouted for joy, opening his arms, laughing up at the sky, which darkened and answered him with sizzling, wonderful bolts of light *(real Earth lightning!)*. When the thunder crashed, Monica, David, and Diane were all awake.

They stayed on their backs, watching the dark sky and its wondrous lightning and roiling clouds; savoring the cool, drenching shower of water; gleefully opening their mouths for it and wiping it from their eyes; laughing, rising to spin in exhilarating circles before falling again to the ground, the mud, the Earth's soft, firm, wet embrace.

Rain, Daniel thought, drinking it in, soaking it in, bathing in it, wallowing in it, dancing in it, laughing and crying in it. Rain and its clouds and its thunder and lightning—he'd seen nothing more beautiful. Not even Earth itself, in its totality, large and blue and white and brown next to its moon among the stars, could match this. This was ancestral wonder; this was the stuff that gave birth to gods. This was the power, the lifeblood of a living planet. Barren or not, the rain still came. With rain, life could again take root everywhere. Centuries might pass, millennia might pass, but the rain—as long as it came—would keep the planet ready.

He rolled, and found Monica in the mud. Her wet hair

fell down, away from her face, mingling with the Earth. Water beaded in her eyebrows, on her cheeks and lips, in her eyelashes. Her wet, slippery body brushed against his. Her lips parted, and she giggled. Her eyes opened wide with joy and wonder, and he kissed her, letting the water run in between their lips, letting her tongue find his, feeling her body sigh against his, press against his, like a flower rising out of the Earth itself.

And then came the light, as the sun burst free of the clouds and filled the sky with color, magnificent arches of color against the blue-gray clouds. They gasped in wonder and rose, dancing through the rain, chasing the color in the sky.

"Look!" Diane exclaimed, stooping close to the ground.

Daniel looked at her, at her clean, glistening body. She could be a statue, too, he thought. Like her father. Her olive-green skin, her long, graceful limbs . . .

He watched Monica and David stoop next to her, and he hurried to wash the last of the dried mud from his skin. They'd found a shallow pool of clean water, brought by the rain and gathered in a depression in a long, wide slab of rock. He splashed the water a final time on his chest and went to join them.

Where Diane stooped, from the moist earth next to the slab, rose a tiny, delicate, purple and white flower.

Monica looked at Daniel and smiled. In the sunlight, he could see the reflection of the little flower in her eyes.

The walk that day was less painful, less tiring as their muscles and bones grew accustomed to the new, greater weight of their bodies.

They slept again in the open. Once, in the middle of the night, Daniel stirred. He thought he heard a distant, rhythmic thunder.

He thought it a dream, and fell back into sleep.

* * *

Early the next evening, they heard the music, distant but clear, grinding guitars, pounding drums, and a bass that made the earth vibrate under their feet. Their eyes filled with tears, and they ran toward the sound. Hope and joy and sadness. Such music—such sounds could mean only *Fiberglass Muskrat*.

Diane fell to the ground then, embracing it, pounding her fists into it.

Daniel pulled Diane back to her feet, and they ran like the wind until they topped a rise and looked down, toward the distant collection of buildings with the huge, haphazard edifice marking one side.

Something hovered, low in the sky over the buildings. As they stood there, on the ridge gazing down, the thing in the sky grew larger, coming toward them.

A flyer.

Daniel held his breath. None of them moved.

An old man with gray hair and young, warm eyes hopped to the ground from the flyer. He stood, facing them.

Just then, a deep, hollow, mournful voice joined the music, and Daniel's eyes filled suddenly with tears. Diane collapsed again, sobbing, to the earth.

The man before them approached cautiously, saying something Daniel couldn't understand.

"She's okay," Daniel told him.

The man stopped and looked at him. "You speak English," he said, his young, warm eyes opening wide in amazement.

Daniel nodded, brushing the tears from his eyes.

"Why are all of you crying?"

"Monk," Daniel said, pointing down at the encampment. "He's alive."

The old man laughed. "What a strange thing to say. Of course he's alive. Can't be killed."

"You must be Genie," Daniel said.

Slowly, creasing his forehead, the old man nodded yes.

"Stigg?" Daniel asked. "Is he alive, too?"

Genie nodded yes again. "Who are you?"

Daniel groped in the air next to him until he found Monica's hand. He fell to his knees, looking at Genie through the swimming tears that he couldn't keep away.

After a time he rose, pulling Monica tight against his side.

"I'm his son," he said.